"You wouldn't have a tick his mom might say.

"It's been Spencer's dream," his dad might add. "It hasn't been yours."

Maybe not, but when did Cameron ever have a reason to dream? Not when they watched Spencer fly off to superselective sports camp. Not when they cheered Spencer's game-winning baskets. Not when they celebrated Spencer's All-School Award.

But since Cameron had an actual ticket in his hands, he felt a spark of possibility. Maybe the Gollywhopper Games were his dream now.

Who would've thought? Not Cameron. Not before that email.

The New Champion

By Jody Feldman

Illustrations by Victoria Jamieson

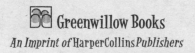 Greenwillow Books

An Imprint of HarperCollins Publishers

The Gollywhopper Games: The New Champion
Text copyright © 2014 by Jody Feldman
Illustrations copyright © 2014 by Victoria Jamieson

Library of Congress Cataloging-in-Publication Data
Feldman, Jody.
The Gollywhopper Games : the new champion / by Jody Feldman ;
illustrations by Victoria Jamieson.
pages cm
"Greenwillow Books."
Summary: Tired of living in his brother Spencer's shadow, twelve-year-old Cameron Schein considers taking an unfair advantage to win the second Golly Toy and Game Company's Gollywhopper Games, in which the brothers and other children compete by solving puzzles, answering riddles, and doing stunts.
ISBN 978-0-06-221125-5 (hardback)— ISBN 978-0-06-221126-2 (pbk)
[1. Contests—Fiction. 2. Games—Fiction. 3. Puzzles—Fiction.
4. Conduct of life—Fiction. 5. Toy making—Fiction.]
I. Jamieson, Victoria, illustrator. II. Title. III. Title: New champion.
PZ7.F3357752Gon 2014 [Fic]—dc23 2014004276

15 16 17 18 19 OPM 10 9 8 7 6 5 4 3 2 1

First Greenwillow paperback edition, 2015

In memory of
the best guide in the world,
my mom,
the original Carol

One Week After
THE GOLLYWHOPPER GAMES

Bert Golliwop had reached a decision. He strode the width of his office—back, forth, back, forth—feeling the eyes of his executive team follow him from their seats around his pool table–sized desk. On his next pass, he grabbed a red file folder, then turned to face the five others. "I don't know whether to curse him or kiss him," he finally said. "That Gil Goodson's going to cost me."

"But he's making us money already," said the chief financial officer. She offered him an accounting spreadsheet. "He was the Gollywhopper Games underdog. The people love him."

"That's the problem," said Bert Golliwop. "They

want to see him. They want to be him. They want to eat him for breakfast. These Games have made him a star, and the kids want more." He slammed the inch-thick file folder to his desk. "Feedback from Fans," its label read.

The Human Resources vice president pointed toward the folder. "Sir? This is . . . ?"

"If you can't read a file label, Jenkins, you're fired."

Jenkins shrank back in her chair.

Bert Golliwop stared at the folder until Jenkins pulled out a few sheets and started reading. The four other vice presidents—Larraine from Finance, Morrison from Legal, Plago from Toy and Game Creation, and Tawkler from Marketing—all followed her lead.

Bert watched from his leather chair, but within minutes he'd had enough. "Well?"

"I don't understand, sir." Jenkins waved the papers. "These kids don't want more."

"Which kids?"

"Here. Jon Inge, eleven-point-five years old. 'To Golly Toy and Game Company.' Subject line: 'Unfair.' Message: 'Why did you pick a cheater like

Rocky Titus and not a fair person like me? I had the exact right answer on the field or close enough. I think you picked people you know. Why should I buy any more of your toys and games? I don't know you personally.'"

"Exactly! I've read that, read 'em all. Read another," said Bert Golliwop.

Jenkins shook her head but shuffled to the next paper. "Subject line: 'Too far.' Message: 'I wanted to play your Games, but my parents couldn't afford the gas to drive me one thousand three hundred and forty-seven miles to get there. I don't think it was fair. Your friend, Meghan Mehadavan, thirteen years old.'"

And the next. "Subject: 'Too Easy.' Message: 'I can't believe you picked stupid people. The puzzles were too easy. Any joker could solve those.' This from sixteen-year-old Kurtis Frenke."

"He was too old to participate," said Larraine.

"He's not too old to buy toys and games. No one is," said Bert Golliwop. "Go on."

Jenkins nodded. "From another eleven-year-old. Subject: 'Too Hard.' Message: 'The stunts were good, but the puzzles were too hard. How could any kid solve those?'" Jenkins looked toward Bert Golliwop with that should-I-go-on? glaze in her eyes.

"Don't you get it, people?" said Bert Golliwop.

"They're not happy, sir," said Jenkins. "Too hard, too easy, too far, unfair, unfair, unfair."

"They may not be happy, but they're jealous, they're talking. They loved it!" Bert nodded at Tawkler.

She tapped at her cell phone, and in came Danny, the new intern, pushing a three-shelf cart jammed with green file folders.

"What's this?" said Jenkins.

Tawkler faced her. "This is gold. And I can summarize all these," she said, running her fingers along the top shelf of folders, "in twenty-five words or less." She read from a note card: "'OMG. I love Gil! Bianca! Lavinia! Thorn! Rocky was fierce! Can Gil visit my school? Be my brother? Be my best friend? Gollywhopper forever!'"

Bert Golliwop crossed his arms over his chest. "Here's the best part. I have it on good authority these Games have that lunkhead Harvey Flummox and his Flummox Corporation reeling. Their toy and game sales, down." It took Bert everything he had to wipe the smile off his face. He cleared his throat. "But that doesn't change what's important. Gil Goodson is going to cost me—you know that, right?—because there's only one thing we can do."

"About what, sir?" said Jenkins.

"About what? About these kids who wrote these emails, good and bad. About making them *all* happy. Just one thing to do."

They responded with murmurs and mumbles.

Bert Golliwop kicked his chair aside, leaned on his desk, the full weight of his body on his hands. "What? What do we have to do?"

Silence.

"People. Are you idiots?" He stared them each in the eye. "We have to give the kids what they want. We need to fix the glitches. We need to go bigger, braver, bolder! We need to hold the Gollywhopper Games! Again!"

CHAPTER 1

Cameron may have been the only one in his family with an actual ticket for their area's Gollywhopper Regional, but his brothers still shoved him to the middle of the backseat like some old forgotten gym bag. At least he smelled better than an old gym bag. He took a quick whiff of his pits to make sure.

"Mom," said Spencer, "he's smelling himself again."

"I'm not doing it in public." Cameron would have turned to stare out his window, but the middle didn't have one and he couldn't keep twisting his neck to look out the back. So he picked at the knee of his jeans, half wishing that his older brother, Spencer, had won the ticket.

It was Spencer who had signed Cameron up—their little brother, Walker, too—in hopes of tripling his own chance to get in. But leave it to Spencer to overlook the rules, especially the one about needing an official ID for arena entry. No normal person would believe that Spencer, who'd been shaving for two years and was nearly six feet tall, was twelve-year-old Cameron. And if Walker had scored the ticket? Nine-year-olds were too young to compete anyway.

Cameron wanted to believe that he was Spencer's oasis in the desert of Golly, his rope in the Whopper of quicksand, his very last lifeline to the Games, that without Cameron's ticket, they wouldn't be driving two hundred miles to his assigned regional. This was Spencer, though, and if he wanted his chance to score a walk-in spot, their parents would drive him anywhere.

"Gil was a walk-in," Spencer had droned on for months. He'd failed to mention that Golly had guaranteed thousands of spots for walk-in contestants last time. This time it guaranteed zero. If one kid with a real ticket didn't show up, though, Spencer had a chance. And if he got in, Cameron, even with a ticket in his pocket, might be left out.

It was simple math: two parents, three kids. No kid could go into the Games without an adult, and their parents wouldn't exactly leave Walker wandering alone in a strange city.

Their mom's old aunt Marilyn lived close enough to the arena to come take care of Walker, but last Cameron had heard, they were still waiting for her to call back.

Maybe Cameron was worrying over nothing. Maybe Aunt Marilyn was available, and they had forgotten to tell him. All he had to do was ask, but why waste his breath? If she couldn't come, it was possible that Spencer would be in and Cameron would be out. He could hear it now.

"You wouldn't have a ticket if it weren't for Spencer," his mom might say.

"It's been Spencer's dream," his dad might add. "It hasn't been yours."

Maybe not, but when did Cameron ever have

reason to dream? Not when they watched Spencer fly off to superselective sports camp. Not when they cheered Spencer's game-winning baskets. Not when they celebrated Spencer's All-School Award.

But since Cameron had an actual ticket in his hands, he felt a spark of possibility. Maybe the Gollywhopper Games were his dream now.

Who would've thought? Not Cameron. Not before that email.

The email had come two months ago. "Gollywhopper Games!!! Confirmed Ticket Notification!!!" Huh? Cameron hadn't entered. Why would he enter something he couldn't win? He almost deleted it as spam, but Spencer stopped him, pushed him out of the way, and celebrated until Cameron showed him the official ID rule.

"No way! This was supposed to be me. *I'm* the one who can win." Spencer sulked all day, until he launched his new walk-in plan. He pulled out his Gollywhopper Games study guide and shoved it into Cameron's stomach. "Memorize," he commanded Cameron. "If I get in, you'll help me." Then he totally abandoned the book like he'd abandoned his hermit crab.

Two days after he'd gotten Crabby, Spencer caught Cameron pushing a kernel of corn toward him. "You love him so much," Spencer had said, "you take care of him. That jerky crab just sits there. Sort of like you."

And Cameron had growled.

"Mom!" Spencer yelled. "He's growling at me, and all I did was tell him he could help take care of Crabby."

After that, Cameron only growled with his door locked and his face in his pillow.

Cameron should have recycled Spencer's notebook, a clone of Gil's study guide from last year. If Golly Toy and Game Company used that info for its questions this year, it'd eliminate only three clueless people. The guide was everywhere online.

Memorizing it, though, gave him momentum to work puzzles, find more Golly facts, and do locked-door weight training with recycled milk jugs he'd filled with water. The only thing he couldn't truly practice was standing up to a thug like Rocky Titus.

He had Spencer around, sure, but Cameron knew how to handle his brother. In the real world, though, against a true bully, he'd dissolve into a shuddering mass of goo.

Did it really matter? He'd never advance enough for that to become an issue.

There were one hundred regionals with 9,999 kids in each. If he were one of the 900 kids from across the country to (A) survive today's regionals; (B) travel to Golly headquarters in Orchard Heights; and (C) join the 100 more who'd received free passes there, he'd still need to beat 990 other kids to make it into the finals. Cameron's odds of doing that were ten in a million, only slightly better than his odds of meeting the president.

Apparently Spencer didn't think about odds. He expected to be in the final ten, and that was possible. Anyone could register at any regional for the Last-Chance Lottery. And if any ticket holders didn't show up, their places would go to the lottery winners.

The moment their dad pulled into the parking space in the arena garage, Spencer shot out of the car and raced down the stairs. By the time the rest of their family caught up with him, he'd navigated around the block and through the thick crowds inside the barricaded, pedestrian-only streets and walkways surrounding the arena. Somehow, he was already eighth from the end of the long Last-Chance Lottery line.

Cameron lagged behind to capture the whole phenomenon on his videocam: the arena, the food tents, and all the activity. "Who knew," he said just loud enough for his microphone to pick up, "that eleven- to fifteen-year-olds came in so many shapes and sizes? And colors." He focused on a girl with red and blue hair wearing a rainbow shirt and shiny gold pants. "Like that's going to give her a better chance to win."

"Maybe she just wants to get on TV," Walker said. Either he had eagle ears or Cameron was talking louder than he thought. "Like Bianca did last year."

Bianca LaBlanc. Cameron and his buddies had decided she must have cast a spell on the other contestants to get as far as she had in the Games. Or maybe not. Maybe being Bianca was enough. If someone that beautiful had been on his team, he would have been worse than a shuddering mass of goo. He would have been a stuttering, drooling puddle of ooze.

Cameron focused his videocam on a sign with a left-pointing arrow: TICKET HOLDER REGISTRATION. "That's me," he said for his microphone.

He turned to his parents, who were watching Spencer in the Last-Chance Lottery line with that same crossed-fingers look they'd had for months. "He's fifteen, it's his last shot, and he wants it so much," his mom had said yesterday as if reading Cameron's mind. "But you"—and she looked him in the eyes—"you have a real chance."

Of course he had a real chance. He had a guaranteed ticket. He wished his mom had finished that sentence showing some faith in him, something like, "You have a real chance *to win*." Not that he'd have believed her, but it would've been nice to hear.

Cameron tapped his dad's arm and pointed to the registration sign.

"We need to stick together. It's a zoo." But then his dad looked at his watch. "Right." They left Walker and his mom with Spencer and headed around the arena.

"Good morning," said the woman when it was finally their turn at the registration tables. "Or is it afternoon already?" She looked at her watch. "Nope. Ten more minutes of morning. Ten minutes plus an hour till arena doors open. And you are?"

Cameron slid his computer printout and his birth certificate across the table to her.

"Cameron. Welcome." She scanned the printout's bar code, then looked at her computer screen. "You are number sixty-three forty-two."

A girl came from a curtained area behind the tables, waving what looked like a runner's bib—a white rectangle with his number, a bar code, and his name. She handed it to the woman.

"If I were you," said the woman, scanning his bib, "I'd pin this to your shirt now so you don't lose it. And don't bother giving it to anyone else; that person wouldn't get past the front gate. Now smile!" A camera went off. "Face recognition software." The woman affixed an untearable paper bracelet around Cameron's wrist, then one around his dad's. "Once you go inside, neither of you can leave the arena without the other. Good luck, Cameron."

They were the first to arrive at the family meeting spot, a patch of shade away from most of the action. "Let's find them in line," his dad said.

Cameron gripped his videocam. "Can't I wait here?"

"You know how you get turned around in big spaces."

Cameron sighed.

"Fine," said his dad. "Just don't move."

After his dad was out of sight, Cameron held up his camera, waved his arms, and shook his legs. "I moved, Dad. Sorry."

A couple of people looked at him like he was pathetic. It didn't matter. Now he had time to shoot some really good footage without anyone, like Spencer, calling him a geek.

He scanned the crowd with his videocam, taking in full scenes, zooming in on one detail, then out to capture the flavor of everything beyond. The smoke from the barbecue stand. The brilliance of the flags. The squeals of people in awe that this thing they had seen on TV last year, this event—well, they were part of it now. And so was he. So was he!

He had to stop being delusional. No way would he get further than having a bib pinned to his shirt. But that counted for something, didn't it? A souvenir? A movie prop? Something to use in a film about a day in the life of a contestant in one of the Gollywhopper regionals? If he made that into a video, maybe it would go viral. Yeah, right.

He kept his camera rolling anyway. "What am I doing here?" he muttered.

"Getting ready to win the Games?"

He turned, his camera focusing in on . . .

"You're—" He felt his mouth open and close like a starving guppy.

She laughed. "I get that all the time. Isn't this awesome? I mean the Games. I mean even without me having a chance to win this year. I'm Bianca. What's your name?"

He dropped his camera to his side but kept it rolling to capture the sound. "Cameron."

"Hi, Cameron." She reached for his camera, and he did something he never did. He let her have it.

Then she pointed to Walker. When had he gotten here? "Who's this guy?"

"He's my brother," said Cameron.

"Yay! Cameron's brother!" She handed him the videocam. "You have a new job. I love being on camera and your brother's never in his own movies. Am I right or what?"

"You're right."

She turned back to Cameron. "So Cameron, huh? That's a lot of letters."

Just one more letter than in your name, he wanted to say.

"You need a nickname. What should we call you?"

She could call him anything she wanted.

"Not Cam. He was the worst boyfriend ever. His name should've been Jerkface. Something else, some other name. What about Ron? Ronny? No. You don't look like one." She bit her lip. "I have it! Let's do initials. What's your last name?"

"Schein?" he said, like he was asking her if he was right.

"Shine? Like the sun shines?"

"That's the way it sounds."

Bianca shook her head. "Nah. Not Shiny. And CS doesn't have any rhythm. Ooh. Maybe your middle name!"

"No," said Cameron. "It's Stanley."

"Ugh."

"I know."

"So that makes you CSS. Like 'kiss,' but with a *C*." She shook her head. "You probably don't kiss many girls."

You think?

"Not yet, I mean," she said.

Huh?

"Oh, you will be hot one day. Those lips will get some action."

Could he turn any redder?

"Look at you with those green eyes, hiding behind all that curly hair. And you're smart, right?"

"He is," said Walker, still holding the camera.

Bianca smiled even bigger, then looked beyond Cameron's camera to the professional one that had been filming them the whole time. "I have a feeling about this guy," she said. "His name is Cameron Schein. You need to watch him. He's going to be hot one day. Right now he's just preheating."

A woman came up. "Time to go, Bianca."

Bianca held out her hand. "Sharpie, please?"

The woman handed her the marker, and she stepped over to Walker. She steadied her hand on his and signed the camera: *Bianca LaBlanc.*

"Ready now?" said the woman.

Bianca held up a finger. "Both cameras are rolling, right?"

She paused to make sure. Then she planted a big kiss on Cameron's cheek. "A kiss for luck." Then she gave him a hug. "This is not for the cameras," she whispered, "just for you. I'm rooting for you, and I don't say that to everyone." She pulled back. "Good luck, Cameron Schein. See you in Orchard Heights."

And for a minute Cameron believed every word she said.

CHAPTER 3

"You what?" said Spencer, death-clutching his Last-Chance Lottery card.

Cameron pointed to the lipstick lips on his cheek, then to the signature on his camera.

Spencer shook his head. "First you win my ticket. Then Bianca kisses you. Next thing you'll be promoted to king of England."

They didn't live in England, and kings don't exactly get promoted, but Cameron wasn't going to stop Spencer's rant. It was too much fun to watch.

"Which way'd she go?"

Walker pointed behind him. "Thataway."

Spencer turned on his heels to race after Bianca. He came back about fifteen minutes later. "How'd you talk to her? She was surrounded by a million people."

Cameron shrugged. "She wasn't here, and then she was."

Spencer held out his ticket to Cameron. "Touch this. Just for a second. Just for luck."

Cameron brushed his fingers over it.

"No," said Spencer. "Really rub it."

If Cameron had rubbed any harder, it would've ignited. At least Spencer wasn't sulking anymore. When Spencer sulked, he wanted everyone to suffer.

The day Cameron got his guaranteed ticket and Spencer got nothing, it had been like a historic moment. Cameron printed out his confirmation and wanted to wave it in Spencer's face, but he didn't. Still, Spencer tore it up. Again, Cameron printed and Spencer tore.

"Cut it out," Cameron said.

"Make me."

That was about as possible as leaping over the house. Instead, Cameron set the printer to make one hundred copies, hoping Spencer would get tired.

Spencer got tired all right. He unplugged the printer, ran with it to his room, and locked the door behind him.

If Cameron had picked the lock, Spencer would've found a way, as usual, to make something Cameron's fault. "Mom!" he'd have yelled. "Cameron broke the printer, but don't worry. I fixed it." He'd have come out golden again.

Not that Cameron needed the confirmation sheet right then, but he wanted that page in his hands.

Cameron put his mouth to Spencer's door. "What do you want?"

"Everything you win."

"Seriously. What do you want?"

"Half."

To hold that confirmation letter, Cameron would have paid a lot more than half the ten-dollar gift certificate they'd probably give him as they ushered him out of the Games. "Fine. Half of my gift certificate."

Silence.

"I said fine."

A minute later Spencer opened his door just enough to shove a piece of paper out. It wasn't Cameron's confirmation. It was a contract: *I hereby give Spencer 50% of anything I win in the Gollywhopper Games.*

Spencer sailed a pen out the door. "Sign it."

Cameron scribbled *Camden Slide* at the bottom so it wouldn't be legal. It was good enough for Spencer, though.

Spencer shoved out the printer.

"By the way," Cameron said, "the deal's off if *you* win anything."

"Try getting that in writing."

Cameron hadn't bothered. What did it matter anyway? For one thing, Spencer's chance of getting in? Near zero. And second, Cameron's chance of winning more than a measly gift certificate? Near zero as well.

"Attention," came a voice over a loudspeaker. "If you are wearing an official Gollywhopper Games bib, you and your adult may enter the arena."

"Well, this is a real pickle," said his dad. He looked from Cameron to Spencer to Walker and back to Cameron. "I thought everyone would go in after the Last-Chance Lottery. When do you need to be inside, Cameron?"

Like he knew?

They headed to his registration lady. "We're in a bit of a bind," said his mom. "We have one adult per kid plus one kid left over and we don't know whether or not the other one will get in and that's not making any sense, is it?"

The woman shook her head.

"What we need to know is this," said Spencer, taking over. He pointed at Cameron. "Does he need to go in right now, or can he wait until I win a walk-in spot?"

The woman looked at Cameron. "Doors close five minutes after we identify all the Last-Chance Lottery winners. Be inside by then."

Cameron held back a growl. Strains of music leaked from the arena. Streams of people flooded the entrance. Cameron was ready for the party, his invitation was pinned to his chest, and old Aunt Marilyn was nowhere in sight.

"I'm getting inside some way," said Spencer.

Cameron didn't bother to tell him about the face recognition program.

"Hey, Mom," said Walker, "if you'd had me one year and eight months sooner, maybe we'd all go in."

"You'll have fun with Aunt Marilyn. She has pinball machines at her house. If Spencer's not in, the three of us will take her to lunch, then go play mini golf or see a movie."

"Aunt Marilyn's coming?" Cameron blurted out.

"On her way," said his mom. "What did you think?"

"Nothing. I just thought if Spencer got lucky and Aunt Marilyn couldn't come, I'd be waiting out here with you and Walker."

His mom laughed. "You need to stop worrying about things like that."

Maybe so, but if . . .

Did Cameron really want to focus on that? Now? He was going in! But when? They waited near a basketball player statue, where Aunt Marilyn was supposed to meet them, every second ticking louder in his head. "What time is it?" he finally asked.

His dad looked at his watch. "Twenty minutes until they start the lottery."

A guy with a Golly Toy and Game Company badge stopped and pointed to Cameron's bib. "If you didn't hear, you can go in now."

"Thanks," said his dad, "but if my other son gets in, we want to find him. No cell phones allowed, you know."

"Wait if you want," said the guy, "but you won't sit with him. Walk-ins have a separate area. If I were you, I'd find a seat near the walk-in section—two twenty-six—and watch the lottery process on the big screen."

His mom nodded. "She'll be here any minute."

His dad nodded. "We'll be in two twenty-seven," he said.

Cameron headed toward the music.

It was a rock band, the first live band of any kind Cameron had heard outside his school's clashing mess of clarinets, tubas, and his own decent trumpet notes.

His hands craved to hold his videocam—to zoom in on the guitar picks and the drumsticks and the fingers beating time on the mic—but he'd had to check the camera at the door along with his dad's cell phone and watch. Golly people were bar coding and storing pretty much everything except underwear. Even hearing aids and eyeglasses went through special scrutiny after reports, last year, of transmission/ receiver devices.

In the next line, a mom had raised a big stink about handing over her purse, but the guard said, "If you don't want your child to compete, that's your right." She handed it over.

By the time they got to section 227, the whole world knew to wait there. In 225, too. Instead, Cameron and his dad moved to an emptier area with a better view of 226.

Cameron's attention, though, was riveted to the live feed of the band on the four-sided video screen suspended from the ceiling. His guessing game—Which Angle Will They Show Next?—came to an abrupt halt when the band finished its last song and the video screen switched to live shots of the audience.

People jumped and screamed when they saw themselves and went even crazier when Golly workers ran on, cleared the band's equipment, then divided the seating areas with orange construction fencing into sections A, B, C, and D. The only difference from the original Games? Chairs now filled the arena floor. Where would the announcer stand?

Apparently, he wouldn't. "Around the country,"

boomed a voice over the speakers, "in one hundred arenas from Alaska to Florida, from Hawaii to Maine, at the exact same moment, it's the Gollywhopper Games Last-Chance Lottery!"

Cameron cheered with everyone else.

"We switch you to local coverage, where you'll watch as lottery cardholders learn their fates. I'm Randy Wright, your voice of the Gollywhopper Games. See you soon."

The screen divided into a tic-tac-toe board showing nine shots from outside the arena. The center square faded out. On popped Bianca.

Cameron wanted to stand and shout, "She kissed me," but no one would believe him, no one would care, and he didn't want to hear a ton of people say, "Me, too!"

"Hi, everyone!" Bianca beamed, and the whole place exploded.

When Cameron didn't think it could get any louder, the lights went down, and a spotlight hit a glitzed-out mini hot-air balloon that descended, then hovered. From inside, Bianca waved, her white-blond hair catching a breeze.

"Welcome to your Gollywhopper Regional," she said over the cheers. "I'm Bianca LaBlanc, and I get the lucky job of being your local announcer. Three of my friends are at other regionals across the country. Lavinia, Thorn, and Gil!"

The video screen showed four of the finalists from last year, everyone except Rocky, the kicked-out cheater. They each said hi, then popped off the screen, leaving only Bianca.

"I love these regionals," she said, "because not everyone has a cousin like Curt, who drove me all the way across the country to do the Games. I heard about this girl who didn't have a driver's license but started driving herself when her mom wouldn't take her, except that was dumb because without her mom she wouldn't have had an adult, so—"

Bianca held her hand up to her ear. "Yeah. They're saying, 'Stick to the script, Bianca.' But I'm not such a good script person. I'll try, though. Okay?"

The decibel level soared and didn't die down until Bianca started talking again.

"At this very minute we're holding at least one Gollywhopper Regional in each state—one hundred regionals in all, but do you really want to know that?"

"No!" yelled the crowd.

"You want to know which people out there are coming in here. Am I right or what?"

To the roar of cheers, the eight squares surrounding Bianca showed kids running their Last-Chance Lottery cards through scanners. Some looked ready to cry when a red light came, but the girl who got a green light started screaming.

"Woo-hoo! She's in!" said Bianca. "So are—" Bianca touched her headphone. "The people in my ear say three hundred ten others will get green lights, and they will sit . . ."

It seemed everyone, including Cameron, pointed to the vacant section in the corner.

"Fooled you!" said Bianca. "Okay, yeah. Most of them will sit there, but the rest are so, so lucky. They get floor chairs. You wanna be lucky, too? You want to sit on the chairs?"

"Yeah!"

Bianca laughed. "How do you know it's not bad luck?"

The crowd quieted fast. "Of course it's not bad

luck." Bianca chattered on. "Unless you cheat to get there, and then you're outta here faster than um, um, something really fast. And yeah. Script. So we have all these cameras and people watching you. When I say, 'Go,' look only under your own seat, and peel off the piece of red tape. Go!"

Cameron peeled off his tape. It was just a piece of tape. So was his dad's. But the guy in front of him had a green token. He jumped and hooted. Then he jumped and hooted again when Bianca told all the green-token people to run to the arena floor.

"Maybe they're trying to make it less crowded?" Cameron's dad said.

Cameron shook his head. It wouldn't be like Golly to have people win something without winning *something*.

The video screen switched back to the Last-Chance Lottery.

"There it is again!" said his dad. "C'mon, Spencer! Next year he'll be too old, you know."

And next year Golly wouldn't necessarily have the Games. Anyway, where had "C'mon, Cameron!" been before he'd peeled his red tape?

Cameron curled the fingers on his left hand into a mock camera lens, held it to his eye, and panned the arena as if he were filming. There were kids racing up the stairs, stairs running alongside the seats, seats climbing to the rafters, where panels of billowing fabric contrasted with the harsh metal of the catwalk and the supports that held the video screen. He really did want to make a movie of his experience. Maybe if he found pictures online just like this, he could manipulate them and—

He dropped his hand. There was Spencer on the screen with his mom and Walker and Aunt Marilyn. He poked his dad and pointed.

"Fingers crossed?" said his dad.

Cameron didn't answer and didn't cross his fingers.

Spencer's ticket went in. The light turned green, then flashed really fast.

"What the—?" said his dad.

A Golly worker handed Spencer a green token. Not only was he in, but the fast flash sent him to the chairs. Was it really a surprise that Spencer had beaten the odds again?

Spencer threw his hands triumphantly over his

head. His dad grabbed Cameron and gave him a hug. "He did it! He got chairs!"

What had Cameron done? Rubbed all his luck onto Spencer and kept zero for himself? Still, Spencer down there meant he wasn't up here in Cameron's face. And splitting his winnings? Not anymore now that Spencer had won, at least, his own gift certificate.

Soon the nine squares on the video screen morphed into a single picture of Bianca holding her microphone. "Congratulations to the three hundred ten contestants who just walked in. And now I have one question for you: Are you ready?" she called.

"Yeah!"

"I said, 'Are you ready?'"

Cameron didn't know if he could yell any louder.

"Let's play the Gollywhopper Games!"

CHAPTER 5

Had it taken this long for University Stadium to quiet down last year? It sounded as loud as a lawn mower chewing a buzz saw, as 1,000 cats having their tails smashed, as 9,999 kids plus that many adults getting all crazy for the Games.

Cameron didn't want to be one of those wimpy hushers who tried to quiet the crowd, but when Bianca held her finger against her lips and shhhed everyone, she just looked beautiful.

It was like someone hit the mute button with a giant remote.

"So I really wanna ditch my script and talk, but they told me I get a little sidetracked like the time in

Austin when it was really hot and—" She laughed. "Sidetracked! So I need to say good-bye for now. But live! From University Stadium in Orchard Heights! The voice of the Gollywhopper Games! R-R-Randy Wright!"

The screen cut to a shot of the deserted stadium. The camera panned up empty seats to a broadcast booth where Randy Wright was holding a microphone. "This was the action-packed setting for the Games last year," he said. "And it will be again, next week, when it fills with one thousand contestants. Will one of them be you?"

Cheers rolled around the arena.

"These Games will test your skill, wits, and careful attention to instructions. Follow them. Exactly. They will appear on your video screen as I speak."

The words were already flowing.

"First, to the seven hundred and eighty-four contestants on the floor . . ." Randy Wright's voice trailed off to pause for the cheers from below.

Cameron focused on "784" pulsing from the screen, his new least favorite number.

"It's your lucky day. Sit tight in your seats for the

next twenty minutes, and you'll skyrocket to question two. That's right! You get a free pass for the first question."

Everyone in the stands moaned except his dad, who smiled and pointed to Spencer and their mom.

The people on the arena floor shouted and jumped and—

"Are you in your seats?" Randy Wright asked.

—they sat instantaneously.

"Hey, hey!" said Randy. "The only thing predictable about these Games? They're unpredictable. The people on the floor got lucky with question one, but if you're still here for question two, advantage goes to you and you alone."

The cheers quieted as Randy Wright explained the same musical chairs format they'd used last year. A multiple-choice question with four possible answers would appear on the video screen. Decide which one was right, head to the concession area, and walk (not run; runners get eliminated) to whichever lettered section—A, B, C, or D—matched the answer.

Unpredictable? Not yet. But that was okay.

Predictability meant fewer worries to cram Cameron's mind.

"Let's get this party started." Randy Wright kept talking through the cheers. "While it's inevitable you will talk among yourselves, we strongly request, adults, that you let your contestants take the lead in answering the questions. And now, question number one!"

His words scrolled onto the video screen as he spoke.

"In last year's Games, we based the first question on Golly's very first board game, The Incredible Treasures of King Tut. This year our first question is just as appropriate: What toy made its debut to mark Golly's first anniversary?"

Too easy! It was info Cameron himself had added to Spencer's notebook. The GollyRocket. Launching Golly Toy and Game Company into its second year. But everyone would know that.

"Answers: (A) something Yuri Gagarin would have liked; (B) something I. M. Pei would have liked; (C) something Jane Goodall would have liked; (D) something Dr. Patricia Bath would have liked."

Huh? The only name Cameron recognized was

Jane Goodall, and outside of picturing her kissing a chimp—if that was even her—he wasn't exactly sure what the woman had done. Did she raise the chimps that had flown in space?

"Do you know the toy?" asked his dad.

Cameron nodded. "It was in the notebook."

"Spencer's notebook? Terrific!"

A small growl escaped. Cameron covered it with a cough and a question: "Do you know the people in the answers?" It felt sort of wrong to ask his dad's help, but Cameron *was* taking the lead, and all the other kids were talking to their adults. "Like, who's Yuri Gagarin?"

"Some Soviet guy, but I can't remember why he's famous. I. M. Pei, though? Architect. I'm sure of that. And didn't you study Jane Goodall in school, Cameron? I know Walker did. I helped him with his report last year."

That was where he'd seen her kissing the chimp, in a jungle, not in space. Cameron stood.

"You know the answer already? Which one?"

Cameron didn't want to broadcast anything. He stayed silent, hoping his reasoning was right, that

Patricia Bath was a medical doctor and not a doctor of rocket ships. He led his dad out of section C, into the concourse, past section D, and into section A, where a line of people about twenty deep waited in one of the entrance tunnels. Great. Did this mean the answer was obvious to every one of the 9,999 (minus the 784 on the floor)?

"It's crowded but not jammed," said his dad. "Are you sure you're right? If you are, it'll be great. We can work as a four-person team on the next question."

"I'm sure," he said. Three-quarters sure. He motioned his dad to bring his ear closer. "The toy was the GollyRocket. And if the other people were an architect, an animal person, and a doctor, then Yuri had to—"

"That's right! He was the first human"—his dad lowered his voice—"in space!" And he actually tousled Cameron's hair.

Section A was definitely more crowded than the others, but they found empty seats in the upper tier.

"Attention!"

Cameron jumped.

"You have five minutes," said Randy Wright.

"Five minutes to be in your section."

Five minutes until sections B, C, and D were gone. He was sure. Almost. Even more sure now that so many people had crowded into section A. They were standing in every aisle plus the walkway between the upper and lower tiers.

Still, when the clock counted down the five, four, three, two, one, he could hear the blood pulsate in his ears.

"And now," said Randy Wright, "the incorrect answers will disappear one by one.

"Good-bye to the conservationist best known for her important work with chimpanzees." Answer C flashed off the board.

"So long to the architect whose accomplishments include the pyramid at the Louvre in Paris and the Rock and Roll Hall of Fame in Cleveland." I. M. Pei's name was gone.

"Now we're down to two. But who might have most liked the toy in question? Was it the first human in space? Or the person who invented tools that restored eyesight to millions?"

A drumroll came over the speakers. The

screen went blank. Then across it flew a cartoon GollyRocket that landed on-screen above both the remaining choices, Yuri Gagarin and Dr. Patricia Bath. The names flashed and flashed fast until only one remained: *Yuri Gagarin*!

Somehow, over the jumping and cheering, including Cameron's own, he heard Randy Wright thanking Patricia Bath for her work, which had helped restore his own mother's sight, then instructing the people in sections B, C, and D to exit. "You won't go away empty-handed. You'll receive a ten-dollar gift certificate for any Golly toy or game plus a chance to win ten thousand dollars. To enter, watch *The Gollywhopper Games* when it appears on TV. One contestant from each of the hundred regional sites will win for a total giveaway of one million dollars!"

Even the losers cheered. As they left, Randy instructed everyone else to stay where they were or face elimination.

Cameron wouldn't move. Cameron wouldn't even twitch a finger if Randy Wright told him he shouldn't. When it came to his family, he was tired of feeling like the third rower in a two-man kayak or the fourth leg on a tripod or the fifth wheel on a wagon or the sixth side to the Pentagon or the seventh muscle in a six-pack or the eighth dwarf, especially when Spencer was around.

If Cameron could be one of nine to make it from this arena to Orchard Heights, he'd be happy. Even if Spencer came with him and even if he got eliminated there immediately, he'd still be happy. As long as he wasn't number ten today.

CHAPTER 6

With three sections of people gone, it was quieter for a minute.

"Those of you in winning section A"—Randy Wright paused for the cheers—"stay where you are. But you on the arena floor, attention! Turn toward section C."

Cameron and his dad laughed at the ones who practically twirled in circles, looking for C.

"In an orderly fashion—no pushing or shoving or otherwise running people over—find your way to any seat in section C."

That was apparently impossible without a mad scramble, but the Golly people kept order and removed the chairs.

"And now, to give the rest of you some space," said Randy Wright, "if you are standing in the aisles, please move to section D. If you are currently seated in an odd-numbered row, please move to section B."

Cameron's dad shook his head. "Guess we're not joining your mom and Spence."

Cameron coughed to shield his smile.

When everyone was settled, Golly people in sections A, B, and D passed out golden envelopes marked *ROUND 2 ADVANTAGE! DO NOT OPEN UNTIL INSTRUCTED.* Cameron wasn't the only one to hold his envelope to the light. Not even the ghost of a word shone through.

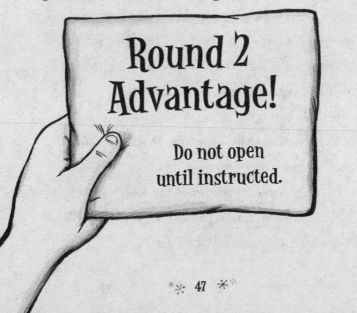

But then the murmur level rose. Golly people were taking down the orange fencing. Within minutes, though, they'd redivided the arena into six sections instead of four.

"It just got harder," said Randy Wright. "We now have six sections for six possible answers. You know the drill. I will read a question. This time, however, I will not read the answers. They will appear only on your screens. You will have ample time to find the section that matches your answer.

"On my signal, open those envelopes and get your hint."

Almost no one cheered.

"Yes," said Randy Wright, "a hint is not as good as a free pass, but it could make the difference. Good luck!

"Question number two! Who were the five finalists in last year's Gollywhopper Games?"

Really?

"Who would need a hint for that?" his dad said, echoing Cameron's own thoughts.

Then the choices came onto the scoreboards.

A. Gil Goodson, Lavina Plodder, Bianca LaBlanc, Thorn Dewitt Formey, Rocky Titus

B. Gil Goodson, Lavinia Plodder, Bianca LaBlanc, Thorn Dewitt-Formey, Rocky Titus

C. Gil Goodson, Lavinia Plodder, Bianca LaBlanc, Thorn Dewitt Formey, Rocky Titus

D. Gil Goodson, Lavina Plodder, Bianca LaBlanc, Thorn Dewitt-Formey, Rocky Titus

E. Gil Goodson, Lavinia Plodder, Bianca LeBlanc, Thorn Dewitt Formey, Rocky Titus

F. Gil Goodson, Lavina Plodder, Bianca LeBlanc, Thorn Dewitt-Formey, Rocky Titus

Huh? They were all the same. Or not. His throat grew cold.

"What the—" Cameron's dad stopped himself. "Ah, spelling! That's great for Spence!" Then he looked down at Cameron. "But not as great for you."

Gee, thanks, Dad. Cameron opened the envelope. Maybe the hint would help.

If Golly was the first to hold an international marbles championship, then Thorn's last name will be alphabetized closer to the name of the country that = fish part + acreage.

If Golly was NOT the first to hold an

**international marbles championship, then
Thorn's last name will be alphabetized closer to
the name of the country that = lion's house +
Huckleberry's creator.**

His dad was reading over his shoulder. "They call
that a hint?"

Cameron shook his head. How could that mess of
words help him at all? But Cameron again looked at
the hint, then at the six choices. He smiled, but he'd
need to talk this out. He leaned closer to his dad's ear.

"Remember how Bianca signed my camera? She
put a smiley face in the first *A* of LaBlanc. L-A
Blanc. So E and F are out."

His dad nodded. "And the hint?"

"I never read anything about a Golly marbles
competition. There was a tiddlywink one and a hopscotch something, but no marbles. So it's the second
hint. And if a lion's house is—"

"A den," said his dad half a beat before Cameron
did. "Plus Huckleberry. Finn, I assume which—"

"Is Mark for Mark Twain," Cameron said before
his dad could.

"Denmark," they both said together.

"Which means Thorn is a hyphen," Cameron said.

"Hyphen?" His dad looked at the scoreboard. "Oh, his last name." He shook his head. "How do you notice little things like hyphens but can't remember spelling?"

Why'd he rub that in again? It had been two instances in fourth grade: a spelling bee he'd flubbed because he'd gotten stage fright and one D on one test, only because he'd forgotten to study.

"I do remember about hyphenated last names. They get alphabetized with the first last name because Alli Schindler-Davis sits next to me when they put us in alphabetical order."

"Good," said his dad. "That knocks out two more answers. So B or D?"

Cameron stared at B, then at D. They were exactly alike.

His dad's tapping foot was as calming as a ticking bomb. So was his pushing Cameron's shoulder and pointing to where Spencer and his mom had been. "They're gone. I'll watch to see where they resurface, and we'll go there."

Cameron wanted to live or die on his own. If he copied off Spencer, he'd never hear the end of it. B or D? B or D? He had to hurry.

He read B softly: "'Gil Goodson, Lavinia Plodder, Bianca LaBlanc, Thorn Dewitt-Formey, Rocky Titus.'" Then D: "'Gil Goodson, Lavina Plodder, Bianca LaBlanc, Thorn Dewitt-Formey, Rocky Titus.'"

"This will serve as your five-minute warning," said Randy Wright.

He had to hurry. But hurrying wouldn't help. Cameron put the mock lens of fingers to his eye and focused on each syllable of B as it came into view. It looked right. Now, if only D wouldn't. "Gil. Good. Son. La. Vin. Ee. Uh." Stop! That's not what it said. They'd left out the *i* in Lavinia! It said *Lavina*. Cameron stood. "Dad! Let's go!"

CHAPTER 7

"**Y**ou're sure we shouldn't wait until we see Spencer?"

"No time." Cameron kept walking.

When they got inside section B, his dad's radar eyes went straight to the third row, and his legs followed. He sprinted down, kissed their mom, then grabbed Spencer in a headlock, ruffling his hair. "I knew you'd get it right!"

If that meant his dad thought Cameron was right, where was *his* headlock?

"How'd *you* get it right?" said Spencer.

"I used the hint and reasoned it out."

"Only spelling-challenged wimps needed a hint for that question."

"Wimp" might have been the nicest name Spencer had ever called him.

While the three of them had a happy family reunion, Cameron watched the people in the other sections, the ones about to leave. He hoped. Worst case? He and Spencer would head home together. But how often was Spencer wrong? Almost never. And not now.

Cameron jumped with his family. He high-fived strangers. He let loose until reality reminded him that hundreds and hundreds of people could still beat him. He sat.

"Are you okay?" asked his mom. She felt his fore-head as if he might have a fever. "You look flushed."

"Just excited." He wished he had his camera to record the girl over there giving raspberries to the other five sections. Or that girl with the hiccups. Or that boy springing from row to row on armrests until a Golly person stopped him.

The people in the losing sections had barely left with their twenty-dollar Golly gift certificates and their chances to win ten thousand dollars when Randy Wright's voice rocked the arena again. "You're still here!"

More cheers.

"Listen carefully, contestants, because I will give these instructions only once.

"You all deserve a break. Bathroom break, food break, stretching break, whatever break you want to take. All the food in the concession area is free. Order whatever you'd like. But keep listening because this is vital."

The place grew much quieter.

"Whether you get food or not"—Randy Wright continued—"you must visit one of the concession stands and have a worker scan the bar code on your bib. You will then get a souvenir Games pen and a receipt. Contestants, you personally need to keep that receipt on you at all times.

"Now go. Eat. Then sit wherever you want. We'll start again in forty-five minutes." The video screen faded to black.

Cameron ordered two slices of pizza, an orange soda, Cracker Jack, and Skittles. Miraculously, his mom didn't tell them to get something healthier. Not even when Spencer asked for chicken fingers in addition to his hamburger, hot dog, pizza, and fries.

Cameron shoved his pen, his receipt, and some napkins into his right-front pocket to better balance the cardboard tray with his food and drink. His family found seats in section E, and Cameron snarfed down the pizza with half his soda. Then he dumped some of his Skittles into his Cracker Jack box despite Spencer's "So disgusting." Yet Spencer was dipping his pizza into a ketchup-mustard combo like it was the most normal thing on earth. And he laughed when Cameron had to dig out napkins to wipe sauce that had dripped dangerously close to his leg.

It wasn't long after they'd thrown away their food trash and taken a bathroom stop that Randy Wright gave them a five-minute warning. Three hundred seconds later he came back.

"We know you will talk among yourselves, but a reminder that the more people you help, the more

Gollywhopper
Games
RECEIPT

1000

* * * *

2 - Pizza
1 - Soft drink
1 - Cracker Jack
1 - Skittles

* * * *

Have a Golly Day!

* * * *

Gollywhopper

competition you'll have. Also remember, your neighbor might not be right. With that, let us continue," said Randy. "Assume there was one Golly worker for every four contestants who got a free pass for the first question. How many people were on the floor of your arena during question number one?"

Cameron focused on the screen.

A. 980

B. 1,960

C. 1,764

D. 1,568

E. 935

F. 1,683

Spencer and his mom and his dad were all staring at him. "What?"

"You're the math guy," said Spencer.

They just assumed he remembered the number. Fine. He'd do the math for the family. He pulled his pen from his pocket, but where was his receipt? He checked every pocket. If he'd lost—

There, on the ground with a trampled napkin. Was that it? Yes! He picked it up, sauce smudged but intact.

He shook out his nerves. It was math time. First, his new least favorite number. He wrote 784 on the back of his receipt. Then divided it by 4 because there was one Golly worker for every 4 contestants. Under 784 he wrote 196 and totaled them. There it was! A. 980.

He opened his mouth to tell them where to go. His mom was staring at him. His mom! She'd been on the floor. Each contestant had had an adult down there. He added in another 784. Now he was right.

CHAPTER 8

When they got to section C, a few people were still scribbling on napkins, on hands, on pants, on anything. One girl was fighting with her mom over which was right, D or F. Cameron smiled. Either way, gone! Still, the drama had him gripping his armrests until the wrong answers disappeared.

His parents' whoops drowned out Randy Wright's announcement of the parting gifts, but they quieted in time for his next words. "How many of you are left?"

Cameron wasn't the only one to stand and count.

Randy Wright laughed. "This is not a test. It so happens, there are seventy-three thousand fourteen of you. An average of about seven hundred thirty at each of the one hundred sites from coast to coast to Alaska and Hawaii!"

The screen divided into postage stamp–sized squares of people cheering.

"It's time for the great divide again! All adults, head to section A. You have two minutes to vacate your current section. Go!"

Cameron's mom and dad gave them each hugs.

"You two stick together," said their mom.

"What if we can't agree?" Spencer said.

"Try." Their parents headed out.

Spencer's knees were jiggling up and down faster than the time he'd decided to ask Dana Caine to the freshman dance last year. Maybe he did want this more than Cameron did. Not that Cameron would let Spencer win, but maybe he could stop Spencer's dumb impulses from taking over. Like when Spencer worked up the nerve to call Dana Caine. At six-thirty in the morning. And Cameron had dared to grab the phone away before Spencer'd finished dialing.

Spencer nudged him. Their parents were in section A, waving with giant motions.

"They're a little too happy sometimes," said Spencer.

Cameron laughed. It relaxed him for a moment. Then Randy Wright came back.

"Contestants? You are on your own. Any mistakes will be of your own making. Victories will be yours alone."

Cameron wished.

"Before the next question, you must follow my directions quickly and exactly. First, take out your receipt from the concession stands."

Cameron nearly panicked over what might have happened. Panicked a little more over whether he'd be penalized for having written on his receipt. Or for having it sauced.

"If you forgot to get a receipt, move to section B. We'll take care of you there. If you lost yours or if your adult has it, move to section D."

Several people around him moved toward the concession area. Some others searched their pockets and inside their shoes, then left, too.

"If you have your receipt, please check the number in the upper-right-hand corner. If your receipt has a ten, move to section E. If the number is one hundred, move to section F. If your receipt shows one thousand, remain in section C. Go!"

Cameron and Spencer compared receipts. Cameron's had one thousand, Spencer's, ten, but Spencer sat there.

"Why are you still here?" Cameron asked.

"They only want us to spread out. Anyway, Mom and Dad said to stay together."

Cameron nodded. Um, no. "What if this is a test?"

"Like they're gonna check every receipt."

"They might."

Spencer looked at his ticket, looked at Cameron, and looked across to his parents giving them the thumbs-up. He stood. "See you later. But if I'm right, you owe me an extra ten percent of whatever you win."

"Ten percent of what?" said Cameron. "You'll get your own prize." But Spencer was already too far away to hear.

Across the arena, his parents were standing, palms up, mouthing, *What's going on?*

What was going on? Cameron had saved his

brother. He knew in his gut; otherwise, they wouldn't have made such a big deal over a receipt. When Randy Wright came back, Cameron knew it for sure. The ones who had forgotten to get receipts, eliminated. Lost receipts, out. Left them with adults, good-bye. Then Golly workers came around, checking receipts against bibs, kicking out kids in the wrong sections.

It was an "I told you so" moment if there ever was one. Too bad Cameron couldn't rub it in, but it was better this way. Each of them, as Randy Wright said, was on his own.

CHAPTER 9

The kid in front of him turned around but bypassed Cameron to high-five another boy about six feet away. Several other kids were yammering with their near-disaster stories; Cameron, though, held back.

If he could keep this up, he'd be one of 9—just 9—from this regional to face 991 others. And those others would include Jig Jiggerson.

Jig, last year's first alternate, had gotten nearly as much TV time as the contestants. He was dubbed the Minute Man, ready to jump in if someone got hurt or disqualified. But Rocky had gotten kicked out too late for Jig to take his place. When Golly announced the new season, they also announced Jig would automatically join the field of one thousand in Orchard Heights. It felt like all America had cheered for the guy who missed the cut by one in the desk challenge.

But now Golly people were coming up the aisles, handing each kid a pencil plus a mini clipboard with a bubble-style answer sheet that had two sections: *Bib Number* and

Jig Jiggerson

First Alternate

Answer. Answer had seven columns of numbers, zero through nine. This was a math problem. The desk challenge without the desks! The final question!

Spencer's legs had to be jiggling like crazy. As smart as he was, he froze at math word problems. For almost a year he'd had Cameron feed him some every once in a while, hoping he'd get immune to them. It had been annoying, but now Cameron couldn't help himself from sending Spencer extra brain waves, reminding him to take one step at a time.

"On your bubble sheet," Randy Wright said, "you'll see a seat location at the bottom. Please find that seat."

Cameron moved three rows down and five seats over, his own knees like rubber.

"You each have a seat," said Randy Wright. "You each have a pencil, a clipboard, and a bubble sheet. And now, instructions." The screen gave a tutorial on filling in answer bubbles; then Randy Wright came back.

"The next challenge will be answered with a number. When you have derived that number, fill in the correct bubbles on your sheet. Note that there are seven columns. Your answer may or may not be seven digits long. If it's not that long, fill in zeros to the left of your answer. If your answer is fifty-one, for example, you would fill in zero-zero-zero-zero-zero-five-one. If you did it the other way, you would give us an answer of five million one hundred thousand. Quite a difference. But you must fill out all seven columns or your card will be rejected by the computer and you will be eliminated.

"Because this round will require some math, you may use the blank side of your card for your calculations. Any marks on the front: computer rejection again." Randy Wright then gave them time to bubble in their bib numbers.

"From here on out," he said after a few minutes, "the directions will be more crucial than ever. So follow each to the letter. Stay quiet. No standing. No kneeling. No leaning. No cheating. And here's the question:

"Take the total number of Gollywhopper Games contestants who started the day in arenas across the country.

"Divide that by the number of arenas involved in the Gollywhopper Regionals today.

"Subtract from that the number of snowflake points in a gross.

"Subtract from that the number of players in the starting lineup on a professional baseball team plus the number of starters on a professional basketball team.

"Add the number of pages in the Golly Dolly instruction book inside each box.

"Reverse the digits in your current running total.

"Multiply that by the average (or arithmetic mean) age, in months, of the contestants left in this competition nationwide.

"Fill in the bubbles to show us that number.

"Time starts . . . now!"

Just like he'd coached Spencer, Cameron told himself, one piece at a time.

Total number of contestants today.

He turned his bubble sheet over and wrote 999,900.

Divided by the number of arenas. Whoever had the wrong answer so far deserved to be eliminated. It was the same number that started in each of the 100 arenas today: 9,999.

The number of snowflake points in a gross.

Cameron loved this. One day Walker had dumped his orange juice and turkey bacon into his oatmeal so he could eat his whole breakfast with a spoon.

"You're gross," Cameron had said.

"No, you're gross," said Walker.

"No, you're gross."

"You know what's gross?" Spencer yelled over them. "One hundred forty-four. That's gross."

Cameron and Walker looked at each other and burst out laughing. Sometime after Walker had thrown that mess into the garbage, Spencer told them that 144 of something was called a gross, and they had called one another One Forty-four until it got old. So 144 times 6, the number of points in each snowflake. He subtracted 864.

Now sports teams. Basketball. Easy. Five. Two guards, 2 forwards, 1 center. Baseball? Nine, right? Three on the bases, the catcher at the plate, the pitcher on the mound, and 3 in the outfield. Eight. Why did he think 9? Where would a ninth guy play? Backing Cameron up, that was for sure. Cameron could swing the bat, but you couldn't count on him to field the ball. So 5 plus what? Eight or 9? One number couldn't keep him out, could it? He subtracted 13.

The number of pages in a Golly Dolly instruction book? That doll didn't talk or pee or fetch snacks. It was Golly's original doll with a zillion different outfits. Trick question? Had to be. There was no manual. He added 0 and circled 9,122.

Reverse it: 2,219. Uh-oh. One baseball player would make a huge difference after all. If a team had 9 players, his running total would be 1,219. Go with 8? Go with 9? Shortstop! Go with 9. He scratched out 2,219 and wrote 1,219.

The next piece would separate them all, and it was anyone's guess. The average age of the contestants. If they ranged from eleven to fifteen, the average would be thirteen. And in months— Wait! Your sixteenth birthday could be tomorrow. You could be fifteen years and eleven months. Cameron wrote down the range of possible months: 132 to 191.

He jotted down 161.5, the average of those numbers. But there'd be more older kids, right? How many just-turned eleven-year-olds would stand a chance?

Should he play it safe: 161.5? His gut was screaming at him. Too young! A year older? Too old! He split the difference: 167.5. He multiplied: 204,182.5.

He reworked the math again and a third time: 204,182.5. Good enough. Except he needed to round it up or down, and he had only a minute and a half to bubble in his answer. Up or down? Up or down? *Ack!* Down. He liked the way the number started with a 2 and ended with a 2. He bubbled in 0 2 0 4 1 8 2.

Cameron exhaled. He'd done everything he could.

CHAPTER 10

The Golly people collected their sheets and instructed them to reunite with their adults.

Spencer caught up to Cameron in the concourse. "What'd you answer?"

"Two-oh-four one-eight-two. You?"

Spencer let out a breath. "Two-oh-four seven-nine-two."

It was scary their numbers were so close. Or maybe good.

"Golly Dolly?" asked Cameron.

"Trick question. All the way."

"Gross?" said Cameron.

"Gross!" And they high-fived.

Cameron loved moments like these when Spencer felt like a friend. "Average age?" he asked.

"Fourteen," said Spencer.

"I went half a month younger."

"Half a month? Seriously?"

And the moment faded.

Inside section A, their parents greeted them with hugs and way too much mush even for sled dogs. Cameron pulled out of their clinches and watched a few Golly people milling around the arena floor.

"I have a feeling," Spencer said, "I'm about to hit victory lane. If I forget to thank you afterward, Cameron, you boring me all these months with math stuff? It was so worth it."

A real thank-you? Sort of. Then you're sort of welcome, Spencer. But wait. Why would Spencer make it and not Cameron? Except for average age, their answers—

"We have results!" Randy Wright's face covered every inch of the screen. "To hear them, we put you in the capable hands of your local announcer. Until Orchard Heights, I'm Randy Wright wishing you the jolliest, Gollyest day!"

The screen cut to Bianca in a locker room. "OMG! You guys were amazing! I don't know if I could've . . . without . . . I mean, okay. Script. I will call out numbers, the ones on your chests, I mean, your bib things. If it's your number, congratulations! Sit tight, and we'll tell you what to do. Everyone else, you rocked anyway. You're going home with a fifty-dollar Golly gift certificate and your chance to win ten thousand dollars.

"Drumroll, please!" Bianca looked around. "We don't have a drum? Okay. If you all want to make a drumroll sound, go ahead, but also listen to the numbers." She waggled a white card in the air. "They'll also appear on the scoreboards. And they are in totally random order, just so you know."

Spencer's knees were bobbling, but only in half-time to Cameron's racing heart.

Bianca called the first number. It wasn't his. It wasn't 6342.

Now what? Golly people were moving chairs back onto the arena floor.

Second number. No.

Nine chairs in one row.

Third. No.

Nine more chairs in the second row.

Fourth. Still no.

For the nine finalists?

Fifth. Crud.

And their adults?

Sixth. Double crud!

Maybe they were setting up for something else today.

Seventh. Spencer? Spencer!

Which would leave only two more spots—

Eight. No.

—for him.

"And number nine," said Bianca. "Four seven—"

Cameron stopped listening. He sucked in a deep breath and joined the family celebration. As much as he wanted to moan and cry, he'd make the best of this. Maybe there'd be a next year for him. Maybe—

"Wait!" shouted Bianca. "I see people getting up! Stop! Sit! Who said anything about calling only nine numbers?"

Cameron didn't know whether to laugh or cry,

so he put every ounce of emotion into yelling with everyone else.

Bianca's voice rose above the crowd noise. "Next. Oh-seven-oh-nine."

C'mon. Call 6342 . . . 6342.

"Three-two-eight-four."

Groans from the guy behind him wearing 3248.

"Six-three—"

Four-two. Please. Four-two.

"Six-three."

So close. But not.

"Oh," said Bianca. "Another six-three. Six-three-four-two."

Did she say 6342? Cameron looked at the board. Rechecked his bib. Or started to. Spencer had him in a headlock. His dad grabbed him anyway. His mom was kissing the back of his head. In public. And he didn't care.

For however long it took Bianca to call the other numbers, Cameron also didn't care that Spencer would probably beat him at whatever they had to do next. Right now, he still had a chance.

CHAPTER 11

On the arena floor: eighteen seats, eighteen kids. What next? Musical chairs?

The one time Cameron had played musical chairs at a birthday party, he'd stunk at it. Even when he was four, he hadn't been pushy enough to win. Not even a single round. Maybe he could become a different person in the next five minutes. Maybe he could become a Spencer and claw his way into a seat. Or maybe this wasn't musical chairs at all.

Spencer had straddled a chair backward and was talking to some girl.

Cameron started to sit next to him, but no one had said to sit. Instead, he circled the chairs, watching

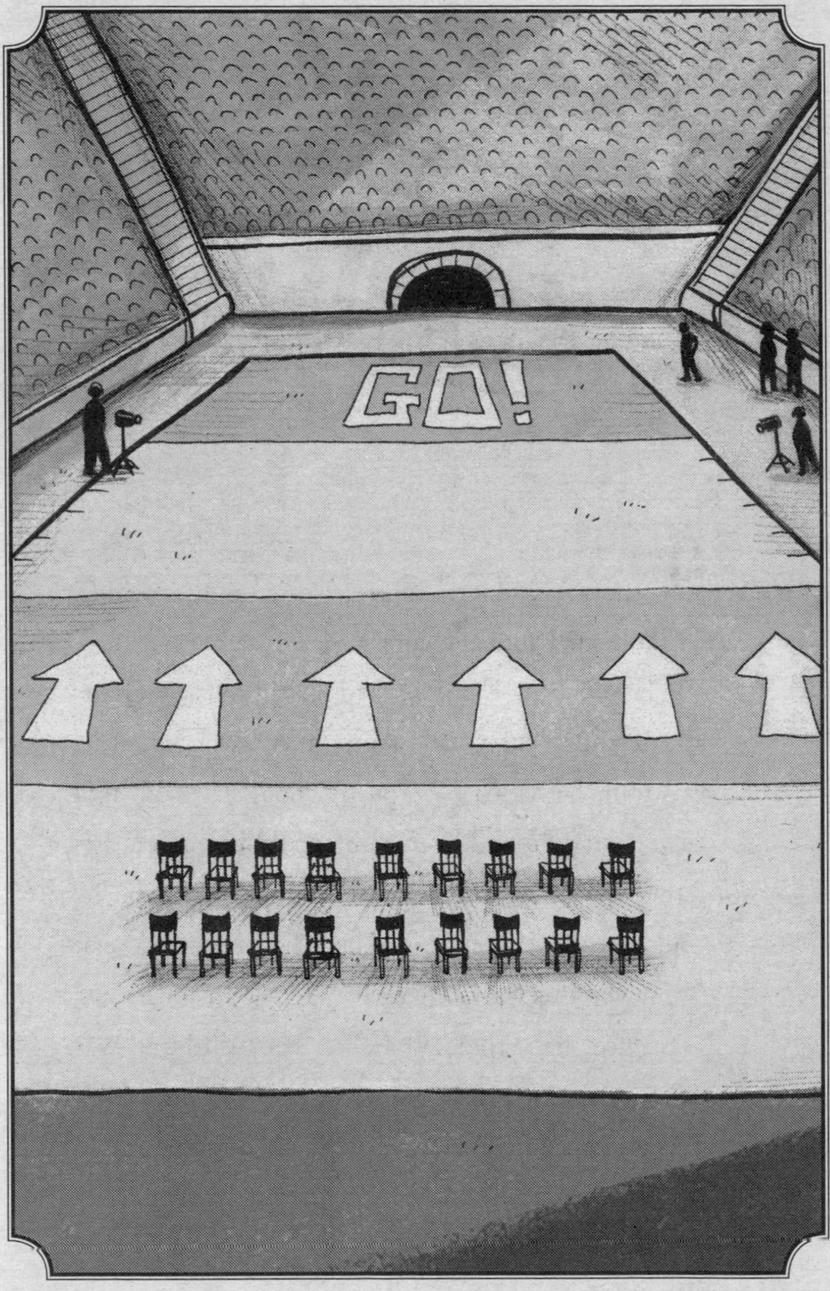
GO!

Golly workers roll out three long, thin mats, each of which ran the entire width of the arena floor.

The mat at the far end had a green line labeled *GO!* The mat in the middle, several feet in front of their chairs, had silver arrows pointing toward the green. The mat way behind them at the other end of the floor was pure red.

Cameron was still circling the chairs when Bianca's voice came back over the speakers.

"Hey, you guys! Congratulations! I'd love to come down and chat, but we have more business to take care of. I've been told I need to read this exactly, so if it doesn't sound like me, I mean the words not the voice, because it is my voice, anyway, you know why. Okay, here goes.

"First, I need you to freeze right where you are. You can relax your arms and get into a comfortable stance, but don't move more than a step until I tell you.

"When I say go, you will run to the end of the arena floor. Just beyond it is a tunnel. Once inside the tunnel, you will find five lit buttons. The first five of you to hit a button will be on your way to the next round of the Gollywhopper Games in Orchard Heights. The remaining thirteen of you will participate in one more challenge. This last arena challenge will determine the other four who will continue playing the Games.

"In a moment I will begin a countdown. When I do, you may start moving again. But until I say go, do not go past the silver arrows in the middle. So far so good? Raise your hand if you understand."

Cameron raised his hand and took the opportunity to unfreeze his head and look around the arena floor again. Where should he go once the countdown started? To the arrows in the middle? Poised to race to the green *GO*? Maybe Bianca would give them more info.

"Good," she said. "I got the okay from Charlie. You all understand. And now for the countdown."

Silence. It was like she was sitting up there, laughing at them all pointed toward the green end. What if that was a fake-out? What if the buttons were at the red end?

"Ten," she said.

They unfroze, and all of them scurried toward

the silver arrows, the few remaining parents cheering them on.

"Nine."

They all were there, Spencer, jockeying for position in the middle; Cameron, a step behind.

"Eight."

This didn't feel right.

"Seven."

Should he alert Spencer? Clue him in? Or just be ready himself?

"Six."

Cameron was here only because Spencer had signed him up.

"Five."

He tugged on Spencer's shirt. Spencer shot him a go-away look.

"Four."

Cameron cupped his mouth to Spencer's ear. "There's another opening behind us. I think green's a fake-out."

"Three."

Spencer looked toward both ends and took a step back.

Cameron turned and started inching toward the red end.

"Two."

"If you're wrong—" Spencer was right behind him.

"One."

If Cameron was wrong, he was already too late to be one of the first five inside the green tunnel. Might as well go for it. He dashed toward the red.

"Go! To the end with the red carpet!"

All right! Cameron picked up his pace, moans and footsteps scrambling well behind him. Except for Spencer, who took the lead. But Cameron didn't have to beat Spencer this time, just be in the top five. Just a few more feet.

Spencer disappeared into the tunnel.

A few more steps. Through the opening. Bright red buttons. Four still lit. Cameron raced to the wall and hit one.

Immediately Cameron felt himself being hoisted backwards, the leverage coming from under his arms. Had some weird Golly gizmo lifted him? No, it was Spencer who had him in the best full nelson ever. "We did it!" Spencer said.

Cameron raised his legs skyward in a foot version of a fist pump. "Orchard Heights!"

"Orchard Heights!" said Spencer.

"Orchard Heights!" echoed the two boys and one girl who had also pushed buttons.

A Golly worker scuttled them out of the way of the other thirteen, the ones who would have to face an additional challenge, whatever it was. Maybe he'd find out; maybe he wouldn't. He didn't care. He jumped and shouted with the four others, all the way through the tunnel, into a room with nine chairs and a snack table.

"Help yourself," the Golly worker said. "We need you here a few more minutes, just long enough for your brief interviews."

Interviews?

"Cool!" Spencer said, grabbing a handful of candy.

"And Spencer, you're first. Come with me."

Interviews? Cameron raised the neck of his shirt to wipe the sweat off his head. Then he opened a bottle of water and managed a sip. For the second time today he'd be on *that* side of the camera. And probably without Bianca to do the talking.

Not ten minutes later he found himself on a stool with lights and a lens targeting his face. He wished he'd brought the water in with him. He wished he were Zeke, the camera guy. His fingers itched to press Record.

"Just relax and talk to me like you're talking to a friend," said Zeke. "If you mess up, no worries. We'll do it again." Zeke smiled. "First question: If you win, what will you do with your million dollars?"

"Um. Well, my brother thinks we're gonna split it fifty-fifty because he's the one who entered my name."

"What do you think?"

"I'm not sure. He's very convincing."

"So what would *you* do with so much money?" Zeke asked.

"I've never thought about it. Maybe I'd save for college or get a camera like you're using."

"You like cameras?"

"Oh, yeah," Cameron said.

"That was good," said Zeke.

"Not too lame?"

"It's fine. Next. If you could have one wish—not money, not world peace—something just for you, what would it be?"

"It'd be nice if people noticed my videos online. They're pretty good."

"I liked making videos when I was your age, and look at me now. Next question, okay?"

"Yeah," said Cameron, kicking himself for not coming up with something more exciting, like zip-lining over Angel Falls.

"Tell me something else about yourself."

"Besides making videos? I guess I'm good at math and I play trumpet, but that's about it." Could he be more boring?

"Okay then. Last question. Which Gollywhopper-eligible kid—family or friend—would be your nightmare competition, a person you would not want to go up against in the Games?"

"That's easy. My brother, Spencer. He knows how to win."

"You mean the Spencer I interviewed before you? He's your brother?"

Cameron nodded.

"Can't blame you for picking him. He has fire in his eyes, doesn't he?"

"Yeah, he does."

Cameron couldn't decide whether to feel proud of Spencer or to grab a fire extinguisher.

The Night After
THE REGIONALS

Bert Golliwop's stare lingered on each of the five executives gathered around his desk. Time to start. "Reports?" He should have asked in a friendlier way, but it had been a long day to end a very long week. "Please."

In turn, the executives reported only minor glitches and malfunctions. A fight over a green coin had broken out at one arena. The audio system cut off for a minute in another. At his location Gil got so mobbed he needed extra security. Lavinia's hot-air balloon got stuck on a catwalk. Bianca kept going off script.

Bert Golliwop turned around to Danny. "You getting all this down?"

"Yes, sir," Danny said.

Bert focused on the executives. "I placed our intern at the arena with Gil. Anything to add, Danny?"

Danny moved to the desk as if he belonged there. "I tried to blend in like an older brother acting as a guardian. You know, T-shirt and jeans, regular college clothes. The place was buzzing like you'd expect. It was great. Except . . ." He looked toward Bert Golliwop, waiting for the green light.

Bert nodded.

"What I noticed," said Danny in a measured voice, "were funky happenstances."

"Funky happenstances?" said Jenkins from Human Resources.

"Unusual activity. One girl tripped over a cord on the arena floor and gashed her head on a chair."

"How is that unusual?" said Plago, from Toy and Game Creation. "Kids trip all the time, especially when they're riled up."

"For one thing," said Danny, "we'd arranged to go completely cordless in the seating area of all arena floors. For another, the cord was plugged into a socket at one end and wasn't attached to anything at the other."

Jenkins shook her head. "Those temporary workers can get so lazy."

"Which has nothing to do with it," said Bert. "It wasn't one of our cords, and it didn't belong to the arena, either."

"Doesn't matter," said Morrison from Legal. "The girl's family can still sue us."

"Got it covered," said Bert. "We sent her straight to the stadium round."

"Which would give us an extra contestant. We have rules," said Morrison, "and with this being on TV, we'll have the FCC all over us. You know the government regulations."

"Got that covered, too," said Bert. "One kid showed a false ID. He's really seventeen, so we already disqualified him."

Larraine inched forward. "Danny. You said happenstances. Plural. What else?"

"None would have been notable without the others, but Gil's microphone package went missing, power was cut to the control area, and I heard rumors that Golly had hand-selected the finalists, that the arena rounds were all for show."

"Balderdash!" said Morrison.

"We know," said Bert Golliwop. "Go on, Danny."

"Like I said, it was easy to blend in." He pointed to the ID on his wrist. "Some parents had received anonymous text messages outside the arena. The texts said the Games were all a sham, so someone either hacked into our system or had the technology to grab their cell phone numbers."

"Beautiful," said Morrison amid several gasps. "Who sent the messages?"

"We checked," Bert said. "They were from a pay-as-you-go cell phone. No way to trace it. And yet they came from the same area code as our good friends at Flummox Corp."

Bert gave them a minute to murmur among themselves.

"You know, Bert," said Morrison. "We can't go around accusing Harvey Flummox of trying to sab-otage our Games."

"He's right," said Tawkler. "He's not our only com-petitor. There's McSwell, Rinky Brothers, United GameCo—"

"But," said Bert, "no one is as clever as Harvey

Flummox." He pushed at the air, trying to shove that thought away. "Regardless, we can't have anyone undermining what we do here. We need to raise our collective antennas and nip all this nonsense in the bud before mischief turns to disaster. Most important, we need to do what we do best. We need to rattle some brains and blow some expectations and put on the best show the world has ever seen! Unless we want to face ridicule."

CHAPTER 12

The whole way home Spencer gave a nonstop play-by-play like he owned the celebration. When he finally paused to breathe, though, their parents took over and teased Cameron. Cameron! How did he know about the red end of the arena? Had he always had ESP? Could he help them predict the next set of winning lottery numbers?

Cameron laughed at the jokes, relieved that he'd been right for two reasons: (A) that he'd bypassed the last arena round, but especially (B) that if he'd been wrong, Spencer would have grumbled forever about Cameron's stupid mistake and how it had made him work harder to outrun all the others, as no doubt he would have.

Instead, Cameron could sit there and smile each time Walker poked him in the arm and said, "Right here in this car are two of the nine hundred winners of the day. What do you have to say about that?" And he'd hold a pretend microphone up for someone to respond.

What would Cameron have to say about that if they faced a wall of reporters and cameras when they turned down their street? Not that there'd be any today, but if one of them won, definitely. The national news had shown Gil's house for three days straight.

When he got home, of course, there wasn't a news truck in sight. The next day, though, Channel 7 was gushing about *another* finalist from his regional as if she'd already won the thing. Cameron's mom said the family had probably sent out press releases. His dad said they'd probably known someone at the TV station. Spencer said she probably paraded around with liver-scented perfume to attract a pack of dogs. It's not that Cameron was looking for publicity, and their mom said it was better if they flew under the radar; but it might have made these Games feel real if the newspaper had run more than one measly paragraph that lumped together all nine winners from their regional.

At least Cameron had the piece of paper to prove it was real.

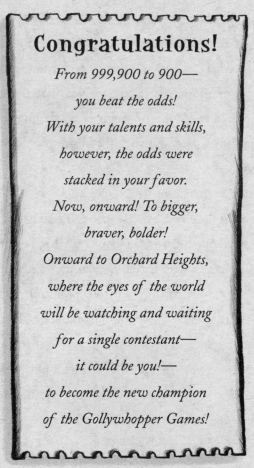

Congratulations!

From 999,900 to 900—

you beat the odds!

With your talents and skills,

however, the odds were

stacked in your favor.

Now, onward! To bigger,

braver, bolder!

Onward to Orchard Heights,

where the eyes of the world

will be watching and waiting

for a single contestant—

it could be you!—

to become the new champion

of the Gollywhopper Games!

For the rest of the week Cameron filmed the note in at least a dozen places—on his pillow, tacked to their house, on the playground slide, wherever he went—always zooming in on the words "*it could be you!*"

Chances were, though, he'd be sent home with the first wave, slapped aside with a flyswatter, squashed like a bug under a steamroller or under Spencer's big shoe. But for now he was headed to Orchard Heights!

And for now he was in a limo, leather seats and all, that Golly had sent to take them to the airport. Cameron even got a window, but that was basically a slam dunk. Spencer and Walker had barged in first and taken the windows in the rear-facing seat. His mom took the middle in his.

His brothers did somehow claim the two window seats in the plane, but Cameron found he could get better interior footage from the aisle. And Spencer only nudged him twice when he leaned over to get a few outside shots. After a minute of being inside the clouds, he had enough fog footage anyway. He doubted, though, he could ever shoot enough of the man near the baggage carousel holding two cards, one with his name and the other with Spencer's.

"How cool is this?" said Spencer. He turned to their parents. "How cool is that? Can I have that card?" he asked the driver as they neared the van.

Jim (his name tag said) handed it over, then gave Cameron his. "Know what, Cameron?" said Jim. "I have a big brother, too. So I'm asking, What's your pleasure? Backseat or up front with me, where your camera can see more?"

Cameron looked at his parents.

"Your decision," said his mom.

Cameron smiled. Maybe things were different in Orchard Heights.

CHAPTER 13

On his view screen University Stadium looked small and unimportant, but once Cameron took the videocam down to see it with his own eyes, the stadium came alive.

Standing behind velvet ropes were throngs of people craning their necks to get a view inside a series of huge white tents sprouting flags and banners. Dozens of mini hot-air balloons drifted in the hot breeze. Walls of video screens flashed colorful pictures of toys and games and moments from last year's competition. Every few seconds a shower of firework sparks soared up and floated down, never really landing anywhere, never seeming to be a danger to anyone.

Jim, the driver, brought the van to a stop on another side of the tents, away from the crowds. A woman wearing a Gollywhopper Games polo shirt immediately opened his door. It was as if she'd known exactly where he was sitting. "Cameron!" She opened the back door. "And Spencer!" she said. "Welcome to Orchard Heights! I'm Sharryn, and I'll be showing you around this place. Derek here will take care of your family."

"You mean we don't get to go with them?" said Walker, climbing out of the van.

Sharryn shook her head and led them to a small lean-to out of the blazing sun. "But we'll treat you like gold; feed you, set you up in a comfy tent, and let you see everything as it happens." She fastened a wristband on each of them. "No one escapes without the other four. You're our prisoners."

"Really?" said Walker.

Sharryn ruffled his hair. "Nah. We just don't want you going where you shouldn't, Walker Schein."

"You know my name!"

"I know lots of things—like . . . Cameron?"

He jumped. "Huh?"

"You'll need to leave your camera here. Nothing comes in except you and your clothes."

"Are you gonna frisk them?" asked Walker.

Sharryn laughed. "No, but every contestant will go through a body scanner like the ones at airports."

"You know they can see underneath your clothes," said Spencer. "Everything."

"Spencer!" said his mom.

Too late. Cameron suddenly felt totally naked. And his face grew totally hot.

Sharryn laughed. "If they could see everything— and I am guaranteed they cannot—they'd see it on you, too, Spencer."

"Works for me!"

Cameron shook his head.

"If you're ready, guys," Sharryn said, "say your good-byes." She took Cameron's videocam and handed it to his mom. "Unless you want Derek to store it in a secure room with your luggage?"

"This is fine."

"Great then," said Sharryn. "Everything's set. Off you three go with Derek. And you two, this way. Ready?"

"Oh, yeah," said Spencer.

Cameron nodded.

They weren't walking that quickly, but Cameron had the sensation that everything was passing in a blur: the tents, the stadium entrance, the concession area—but wait. He brushed his hair from his eyes and looked up. Where were the people? Where was everyone else? He'd seen only about ten other contestants and three other vans. After all that travel, he couldn't be early, and he wasn't late or they wouldn't have let him in.

"You look puzzled, Cameron," said Sharryn.

"What else is new?" Spencer said. "I sometimes think he lives at the corner of dazed and confused."

Sharryn laughed. "Maybe," she said, "but I get the impression there's lots more going through his mind than he lets on. Like maybe he's in shock that one thousand contestants are competing today, but you've barely seen any."

"How'd I miss that?" said Spencer. "Where *is* everyone?"

"No worries," Sharryn said. "I guarantee everything's according to plan."

She led them through the concession area, into a small, carpeted room, and onto one of two elevators.

"Where are we going?" Spencer asked.

"All in good time," Sharryn said. It seemed like her voice lit the button for the fourth floor and closed the elevator doors.

"Is the elevator programmed to do that?" Spencer asked.

"I'd answer," said Sharryn, "but our lips are sealed. Not that the workings of an elevator will give you an unfair advantage, but one comment can lead to another and another, and suddenly the Games self-destruct." She winked.

The elevator opened to a hallway with a bunch of doors. Inside the seventh door down, past a kitchen area, past a couple of TV monitors, past a set of tables and chairs, five other kids were spread out over three short rows of stadium seats. They sat, totally silent, facing a heavy black curtain with a Golly logo.

"Hey, hey!" said Spencer. "So this is what a luxury suite looks like! But what's with the curtain? Why can't we see the football field?"

The other kids turned and looked at him as if

he'd committed the crime of the century.

"It's okay," said Sharryn. "You're allowed to breathe."

A few of the kids sighed.

Sharryn laughed. "As for the field, all in good time. Meanwhile, as soon as we collect a few more contestants, you will start the next chapter of your Gollywhopper Games adventure, and that should happen in five, four, three, two, one."

Just a beat later the door opened, and three girls came through.

Sharryn waved at the Golly person who'd led them in. "Thanks, Wanda." Then Wanda was gone.

Sharryn directed Spencer and Cameron and the girls to their seats, then sat on a large cube to the side of the front row. "Let's do this!" she said. "You probably noticed this stadium round isn't like the Gollywhopper Games of last year. This is a kind of first-come, first-play competition. Some contestants have already been eliminated. Some are still arriving at the stadium. But none of that is important. What is important is this." She stood, opened the cube, and pulled out a bunch of Gollywhopper Games gear bags. "In each of these are pens, paper, a sheet of instructions, and a GollyReader; in fact, it's the GollyReader8, which won't come out for another week. And you get to take that home, but I digress."

Sharryn passed out the gear bags. "First, I will make sure you all know how to use your GollyReader, so no fears if you don't." She demonstrated the basics.

"On my signal, your GollyReaders will come to life. First, you will see an introductory screen with two tabs: Play and Answer." She held up a GollyReader to show them. "Your challenges will be under the Play tab. Solve the challenges, and switch to the Answer tab to enter your solutions. You may go back and forth between the tabs as often as you need.

"Once you are happy with all your answers—there will be five of them—make sure you hit Enter." She showed them. "Then you are done.

"This is a timed challenge. In fact, you are competing directly with the clock and not with anyone in this room. We have preset a time you need to beat in order to advance to the next round. Don't bother to ask what that time is; it's our little secret. But it is possible that none of you will continue. It's also possible that all of you will. It boils down to this: Only those who answer all five questions correctly might move on. Just work as quickly as you can.

"When you have finished, please remain silent and in your seat. Your GollyReader is loaded with some games, just for fun, to keep you busy. In addition, the pens and paper have no hints or information of any kind, but feel free to use them as you'd like. And that's all you need to know for now."

No, it wasn't. How and when would they know if they moved on? What if his GollyReader malfunctioned? What if he himself did?

"I'd ask if there are any questions, but I cannot give you any answers except yes, no, yes, yes, no, and no." She laughed. "Just a very little humor. Sorry.

"Everything I've said is repeated on the instruction sheet inside your gear bag. Take a minute to look it over."

Cameron read through the instructions. Nothing new.

Sharryn cleared her throat. "As always in the Games, we're watching you. No talking, no standing, no neck craning. You won't have time for that anyway. You need to finish fast. But no pressure."

They all laughed.

She held up her hand. "On my count, you will begin. Five, four, three, two, one!"

Cameron's GollyReader flashed "Go!"

He touched Play. There were five questions and a list of twenty-one possible answers.

TO TYPE IN YOUR ANSWERS, TOUCH THE ANSWER TAB.

1. RHYMES WITH A SYNONYM FOR "MORE ANGRY."

2. PARTY FOR A CERTAIN RODENT, PERHAPS?

3. HOMOPHONE FOR A SPECIFIC LANGUAGE OR NATIONALITY.

4. METHOD A STAGEHAND MIGHT USE TO MOVE A HEAVY PROP ONTO THE STAGE.

5. (A) THIS WORD IS IN ITS PLURAL FORM;

(B) THIS WORD DOES NOT CONTAIN THE 18TH LETTER OF THE ALPHABET; (C) THE LAST LETTER OF THIS WORD MATCHES THE FOURTH LETTER OF THE ONLY OTHER WORD THAT FITS BOTH (A) AND (B).

ANSWER CHOICES:

CAULIFLOWER	FINISH	LADDER
CLING	FLAGS	MOUSETRAP
COPPERHEAD	FROGS	ODORS
CRASH COURSE	GEESE	PRONGS
DRAGON	GRAPES	STRESSED
DREGS	HAMSTER BALL	TEMPERATURE
ELEVATOR DOOR	HOGTIE	ZIPPER

There was only one way to tackle this. One question at a time. Number one: *synonym for "more angry."* The only synonym he could think of without really thinking: mad. Madder? Was *madder* there? He skimmed the list. No. Wait. Rhymes with . . .

He looked again. Ladder!

Should he type it in or solve the next? What would take less time? Obviously not worrying about what would take less time. He glanced at question two—*party for a certain rodent, perhaps*—and let that roll around in his mind while he switched to the answer screen.

Rodent party? And what did the "perhaps" mean?

Cameron typed L-A-D-D-E-R faster than he thought he could, which was a good thing, because simultaneously typing one thing and thinking about another? Not working.

Okay, next. Rodent party. He scanned the list for animals. Dragon (fictional, but still), frog, geese, mousetrap. A mouse was a rodent, right? But the trap was no party for mice. Copperhead? Wasn't that an animal? Snake, maybe. Hamster. Rodent? Yeah. Hamster ball. Like those clear balls with doors for hamster exercise. His friend Timothy had one, and his hamster seemed to have a ball in that ball. Was that like a hamster party?

Wait. What about the other definition for "ball"? A dress-up-and-have-a-bow-tie-choke-you party? That was it! Double meanings. That's why "perhaps." The hamster ball could be the pet toy, but it could also be a bunch of rodents whooping it up. Or if a pig went to a hamster ball, he could wear a hogtie, ha-ha! Hogtie. Hamster ball. Puns!

He typed in H-A-M-S-T-E-R B-A-L-L.

Number three: *homonym for a specific language.* For the first time Cameron was so glad his sixth-grade teacher, Mr. Reading, had practically bashed in their skulls drilling in the difference among homonyms and homographs and homophones.

This would be easy. He looked at the list, taking it one word at a time.

cauliflower	finish	ladder
cling	flags	mousetrap
copperhead	frogs	odors
crash course	geese	prongs
dragon	grapes	stressed
dregs	hamster ball	temperature
elevator door	hogtie	zipper

Cauliflower, cling, copperhead, crash course, dragon—

He was just reading. Not concentrating. Cauliflower, no. Cling. Did anyone speak cling? Could a person be described as Clingish like British or Clingan like American? Nah. Copperhead. A nation of people with copper-colored hair? Nope. Crash course, no. Dragon? Sounded closer to American, but he'd never heard of the country Drago unless it was in a sci-fi story. Dregs, like bottom dwellers. Doubtful. Elevator door? That would be funny. Finish. He wished he were finished and on to the next round. Flags—

He was doing it again. Just running through words. Okay. Not elevator door. But finish. Wasn't that what they called people from Finland? And did they speak Finish or Finnish or however you spelled it?

Now he could scan the rest of the list. He paused at every word, but *finish* was the only one that seemed right. He typed it in.

Question four: *method a stagehand might use to move a heavy prop onto the stage.*

Carry? Shove? Push? Pull? Lift? Haul? None of those words was on the list. What was? Zipper? Zip it on? Furnish? Furniture movers? Crash course? Crash into it with a car and have it slide into place. Dragon? Have it fire-breathe the prop through its nose. Wait. Dragon. Drag. Drag on. That was a method, a real one!

He entered that. Now for the last question, a three-parter. First, it needed to be plural. Which words on the list ended in *S*? *Dregs, flags, frogs, grapes, odors, prongs.* Should he write them down? Only if necessary. Second, the word didn't contain which letter? Eighteenth, *R*. That left only *flags.* But wait. According to instruction C, the last letter of the right word had to be the same as the fourth letter of the wrong word. That meant he should still have two words. What had he missed?

Back to the list. The first word. Was *cauliflower* its own plural? Was there such a thing as cauliflowers? Didn't matter. The *R* disqualified it. What else? Another word had to be here. There! *Geese.*

Which word now? The last letter of *geese* wasn't even in *flags*, but yes! The last letter of *flags* matched the fourth letter of *geese.*

Cameron hit the Answer tab and typed in F-L-A-G-S.

Should he recheck all his answers? No. This was a race against time. He hit Enter.

The screen flashed, "Congratulations on finishing the challenge. If you wish, choose one of these games to play while you're waiting."

He didn't wish. He wished he knew if he'd made

it to the next round. He wished he knew if Spencer had. He wished he could stand and pace and not be accused of cheating. He hit the Golly Gobblin' Goblins icon. And he waited.

CHAPTER 14

Cameron gobbled all the goblins in levels one and two. It was better than counting his heartbeats. He clicked Go for level three. The screen faded to black and came back pure green. And with that, a few groans from around the room.

"Okay, then!" Sharryn's voice came from behind them. She raced to the front. "You can breathe, you can sigh, you can move your heads and your arms, which I need you to do right now. Move your arms, that is. I need you to hold up your GollyReaders so I can see the screens.

"Green, blue, and red. Some of each."

"What does that mean?" a girl said.

"It means this. And please keep your GollyReaders held high. Red screen people, you probably know, but your time at the Games has come to an end. Either you did not finish, or you entered an incorrect answer. You can lower your GollyReaders."

"Blue screen people. Good job! You got all the answers right."

Cameron's heart sank.

"However, you didn't beat the clock. Sorry, your time here is over as well. You can lower your GollyReaders. Which leaves us with Spencer, Lauren, and Cameron. Green screens? You're moving on!"

Before Cameron could breathe, Spencer had hoisted him out of his chair. Cameron's GollyReader went airborne, but he managed to catch it before it crashed to the ground. Then Lauren rushed over to join their party. Spencer's excitement must have overtaken his personality because he didn't tell her this was brothers only. Then again, she was sort of pretty.

Cameron pulled away to catch the scene in the rest of the room. Sharryn was ushering the others to Wanda at the door. A couple of kids were crying, one was on the verge, two had that somber but-what-did-I-expect look, and the other two were laughing together.

Cameron doubted he would have cried. No way he'd be laughing, but he could laugh now, all he wanted.

And then he noticed both TV screens in their room. They'd sprung to life with probably a horrifying preview of what was to come. It was a shot of some real objects from this last challenge: a ladder, flags, a human-sized hamster ball, and a dragon-shaped balance beam, plus monkey bars and tires and other intimidating things all set up obstacle-course style.

"I said you almost beat me, Cameron."

He turned to Spencer. "What do you mean?"

"I mean that when I finished, I looked at you with my amazing peripheral vision—have I ever told you about my amazing peripheral vision?"

"Daily."

"Ha!" said Spencer. "Good one. So you typed something, then sat back with that smirk like you owned the world, but I owned it first."

Figured. Cameron also figured he'd hear an earful when Spencer caught sight of the TV screen. But Cameron had seen that first. Ha! Eventually Spencer would notice, and Cameron could say, "That? That was like so twenty minutes ago." Not that he'd actually say it—out loud anyway.

The three of them moved toward the kitchen area, where Sharryn had just finished typing something into her own GollyReader. "Ready to move on?"

"To what?" said Spencer and Lauren at the same time.

Sharryn raised her eyes to the TV screen.

Confirmed. If the next competition really was an obstacle course, mighty ship Cameron was on a fast dive for the ocean floor. There was a reason he ran long-distance track instead of training for the hurdles or the high jump.

"Sorry, bro," Spencer said to Cameron. "It was nice competing with you."

At least Cameron might still have bragging rights: that he was the little brother of a kid who made it to the Gollywhopper Games finals. If that counted for anything.

CHAPTER 15

"All righty." Sharryn turned off her GollyReader. "As you may have surmised, you'll be heading to the football field for your next challenge." She pointed toward the front of the room. "If you were to look beyond the curtain, you'd see six contestants, each running one of six identical courses. This has been going on all day. Each of you will face the course. And yes, you will be timed. We will combine your course time with the time it took you to complete the challenge from this room. The ten with the best scores will move to the finals."

If Spencer had smiled any bigger, his face would

have split in two. It was simple math. Spencer had finished the GollyReader challenge faster than Cameron. Spencer was the fastest runner in their school. Add the two together, and Cameron didn't stand a chance. Sure, there were nine other spaces, but still . . .

At least he could create and post a video ode to Spencer, who would send the link to all his friends, earning the video more than a dozen hits.

Spencer and Lauren were jabbering together down the hall and inside the elevator.

Sharryn smiled at Cameron. "You're quiet, buddy. Overwhelmed?"

He shook his head a little.

"Maybe you're just the silent type."

Cameron nodded. Then he laughed. "I guess that proves it."

"It's refreshing," Sharryn said, "as long as you're not too silent."

The elevator doors opened, and she led them past the stadium concession area and through a door marked "Media Room."

About twenty other kids all turned to see who'd come in.

Spencer leaned over to Cameron. "Competition doesn't look that fierce."

"Don't underestimate anyone," Sharryn said. "And this is where I leave you. There's a chance I will see you later, but if I don't, good luck." She was gone with a wave.

A man in the room closed the door behind them. "And with these three," he said in a voice loud enough so everyone could hear, "we're ready to begin. Are you ready?"

A few kids shouted, "Yeah!" The rest of them were pitifully quiet. Nerves?

"I said, Are you ready?"

That got him the reaction he wanted.

"Quick introductions. I am Hubert Plago, Vice President of Golly Toy and Game Creation. We are the ones who think up, build, and manufacture all the new Golly products. Best job ever, by the way. And this is Rena Jenkins, Vice President of Human Resources."

"Which means, in part," said Rena Jenkins, "that

I'm in charge of the people who do a lot of hiring and firing. So if someone treats you poorly here, he or she is fired." She laughed, but it didn't sound all that funny. "Tough crowd," she said.

Hubert Plago gave her a weak smile. "Anyway, congratulations to you, our fourth group of twenty-four today!"

Rena Jenkins stepped in front of him. "Your next challenge—"

Something like a small explosion shook the room, then there was silence. Part of their next challenge?

Rena Jenkins gave a slight smirk.

"Was that you firing someone, Rena?"

"Um, yes. Um, no. Um, I don't know what that was, but your next challenge will help determine if you are one of our ten finalists. And here are the rules and procedures."

"Rules? Procedures? Who wants those?" Hubert Plago laughed. So did most of them.

Rena Jenkins glared at him. "We need rules here."

Hubert Plago was still laughing. "Of course, of course. So because we *need* rules, we'll repeat what you've already been told. The ten of you who have the fastest combined times—obstacle course plus today's other challenge—are our finalists. It's as simple as that."

"It's not quite that simple, Hubert," said Rena Jenkins. "If you cannot correctly complete a leg of the course, go to the next. You will, however, incur penalty seconds, which will far exceed the time it takes an average person to do the same task. Skip them all, and we add thirty minutes to your time."

Hubert Plago nodded. "And now, that's all, except who wants to go first?"

Several hands shot up. Not Spencer's and not Cameron's, though he wanted to be done with this.

"And who wants to go last?"

Spencer's hand went up.

Cameron looked at him.

"You know I need time to stretch and visualize," Spencer said.

"Sorry to tease you," said Hubert Plago. "You don't get to choose."

Rena Jenkins held up a yellow box. Its top had a hole with rubber flaps. "Reach in, grab a numbered ball, and that will be your order for the obstacle course. Line up. Pronto."

Cameron would've loved to record kids jumping and shouting out their numbers, almost as if they'd won a hundred dollars.

He latched on to ball number five. That was good. No. That was perfect. Enough time to catch his breath, but not so much that his nerves would turn him goofy.

Spencer pulled his ball: twelve. "I need to swap," he said.

It was like Rena Jenkins had superpower ears. "No swapping. You get what you get. Numbers one and two, come and bring your gear bags!" She opened the door, and another Golly person led the two girls away.

"For your viewing pleasure." Hubert Plago pushed a button on the wall, and a large screen came down from the ceiling. "*Looney Tunes*," he said. "Some of my favorites."

The noise was good. Bugs Bunny popping out of his hole, munching a carrot, was still funny. Cameron needed this distraction; otherwise, his expectations would climb and his hopes would soar. Then, when he was sent home, he'd plummet back to earth especially hard. His knees started bobbling.

Spencer leaned over. "With one exception, this room is not filled with sports superstars. You're faster and better than a lot of these people. We're from the same gene pool. Remember that." Then he laughed at Elmer Fudd before he started bending and stretching and pumping himself up the way he did before any game.

"Numbers three, four, and five?"

Already? Cameron made his way toward the door.

"Cameron, Lauren, and Tyler, huh?" said Rena Jenkins. "Don't worry. This is totally painless. Just have fun and follow all the instructions."

"Aw," said Hubert Plago, "who needs instructions?"

They each went out the door with a different Golly worker. Cameron's person ushered him to the left and through the concession area, every step sounding like a slow-motion, amped-up thud.

They came through an entrance to the field. The sunshine nearly blinded him. Cameron blinked hard, then inched open his eyes, feeling for the first time how hot it was outside.

"Take a minute to adjust to the light," the man said.

"Meanwhile, hand me your gear bag. You'll find it at the end." He led Cameron down rows of bleachers and stopped before they reached a wall of towering blue curtains with a slit of an opening. "Beyond this is your obstacle course."

The man pointed to a yellow mat several feet in front of them. "The moment you step on this," he said, "your time begins. Once you're fully through the curtain, you'll see a wide ladder. That's your first stop. Be careful. Be observant. After you reach the ladder, it should be perfectly clear what you need to do next. You may start whenever you're ready. Good luck, Cameron!"

This was it. He took a deep breath, got into his starting stance, rocked back on his right leg, pushed off, and crossed the yellow mat. He burst through the curtain to the sight of more blue curtains encircling an area with all . . . this . . . equipment and all these Golly people.

A ladder. He had to get to a ladder. There it was, ten yards ahead, connected to the biggest set of monkey bars (decorated with monkeys) he'd ever seen. He raced to it, stepped on the first rung, the second. His hands grabbed above him, but the next rung felt different. It *was* different. It was a wooden plank. *Stop!* said the words burned into the wood. *Do not run the obstacle course. Instead, collect 4 flags of different colors, and follow their instructions. In order.*

What flags? Cameron jumped off the ladder. The flags—red, green, blue, and yellow—rimmed the entire perimeter. He raced to his right and grabbed one of each. The blue one said *#2 Hand me to a Golly official.*

He turned toward the official nearest him. Wait. That flag said #2. Which was #1? Yellow was three.

Red! *#1 Plant me in the dragon's right nostril.*

Dragon? There! The dragon balance beam he'd seen on the monitor. He ran and put the red flag halfway in the nostril to his right. No. That would be the dragon's *left* nostril. He planted it in the other.

Turned. Golly official, there, ten steps away! He gave her the blue flag.

The yellow flag was #3. *Put me inside the human hamster ball.*

He sprinted, tossed the flag inside.

Last flag. Green. *#4 Carry me, waving, across the red finish line. It's near the spot where you entered.*

Where had he entered? He was totally turned around. The place was flanked with blue curtains. Which way? Which side? He pivoted, and there it was: a big, red *Finish* sign.

Cameron barged through, but no one was there. Had he got it wrong?

He turned to go back, but his name was blinking on a lighted sign. Underneath, a downward arrow pointed to a table with a gear bag and a GollyReader.

Cameron touched the screen, and the GollyReader sprang to life.

HA-HA-HA! JUST WHEN YOU THOUGHT YOU WERE DONE, CAMERON . . .

TOUCH PLAY.

He did. At the top was the same word list as before. Underneath were two questions.

CAULIFLOWER	FINISH	LADDER
CLING	FLAGS	MOUSETRAP
COPPERHEAD	FROGS	ODORS
CRASH COURSE	GEESE	PRONGS
DRAGON	GRAPES	STRESSED
DREGS	HAMSTER BALL	TEMPERATURE
ELEVATOR DOOR	HOGTIE	ZIPPER

1. SPELLED BACKWARD, THINGS USUALLY CONSIDERED DELICIOUS.

2. WHAT A CERTAIN FARM ANIMAL MIGHT WEAR TO THE HAMSTER BALL.

He could do this. Number one. Not some*thing* usually considered delicious, but *things*, plural, which meant, if you reversed it, the word should start with an *S*. Only one word did: *stressed*. Yes, he was stressed, thank you.

Backwards, though? Desserts.

Question two? Slam dunk. Cameron had solved it even before he knew it was a question.

He switched to the answer screen and typed in S-T-R-E-S-S-E-D and H-O-G-T-I-E.

The screen flashed black before it lit up again: "Breathe. You have officially finished the Stadium Round."

CHAPTER 16

But what did that mean? Where should he go?

The man who had brought him to the obstacle course stepped through the curtain. "Good job, Cameron!"

"Good enough?"

"Don't know. I'm just here to usher you to your family in tent twenty-four. After that, Sharryn, I believe, will let you know the rest. Let's go."

The rest of what? This would be the hardest part. The waiting, knowing he might have a chance. No way he'd racked up any penalty seconds. He'd been fast with *stressed* and *hogtie*. Some kids must have been slower. Some probably ran the obstacle course.

Poor Spencer. He would. Nothing distracted him when he was in game mode.

Inside the tent was a bank of six large TVs, each showing a different obstacle course. He didn't see his mom and dad and Walker until they charged him.

"You were amazing," said his dad. "How's Spencer?"

How's Spencer? They all looked at him as if he were holding Spencer's fate in his hands. They didn't bother to ask exactly how he himself was feeling.

"In game mode."

"Oh, crop-rot," said his dad.

"I was afraid of that," his mom said. She bobbed her head toward a girl crying in the corner. "Didn't see the directions." She shook her head. "Poor Spencer."

They all turned to the monitors. His mom pointed to the second one. "There he is!"

"C'mon, Spence!" said his dad. "Let's hope he flies past anyone we've seen so far."

His mom kept her eyes glued to the screen. "He meant except you."

"Right, right," said his dad. "I meant, he's so fast he has that ability if he sees the plank."

Cameron didn't bother to mention he'd also have to answer those two questions, which they weren't showing on the monitors. Then again, Spencer had finished the other puzzles faster than Cameron.

Spencer rocked forward and back and raced past the starting mat. So fast. He took a flying leap and hit the ladder on the third rung, his eyes already above the plank.

Was it wrong that Cameron gave a silent cheer?

Spencer took the monkey bars two at a time, slid down the chute, ran the hamster ball to the high hurdles, jumped those, high-stepped through the line of tires, raced across the dragon's spine, sped into the tunnel, and did it all in less than two minutes, their dad said.

Their mom had stopped watching.

Spencer had already heard the bad news before he came into the tent. His mom and dad pulled chairs into a little circle and consoled him.

Cameron kept his sights on the video feed. Some kids messed up the flag order; some pulled a Spencer;

some were even more turned around than Cameron had been; most of them ran it perfectly, but it was impossible to tell if they were faster or slower than he had been. For all he knew, he could lose by a nostril, the wrong nostril, where he'd almost planted the first flag.

He'd know something soon. Sharryn was back. She leaned toward his parents. "I need to borrow Cameron," she said. "Wanda will come explain."

Explain what? But Sharryn didn't say. She smiled at Spencer; but his head was in his hands, and he was stomping at the ground.

At least his dad gave Cameron a hug and his mom mouthed, *Good luck*.

Sharryn led him away. "It's tough on him," she said. "I guess in his world the little brother's not supposed to beat him."

"In his world no one's supposed to beat him." Cameron slowed down. "Wait. I *did* beat him. Sort of. I mean, he beat himself. But still I'm—" He kept pace with Sharryn again.

"Those're the most words you've strung together today," Sharryn said as they walked out one tent and into another. "You know, Cameron, I'd often love more silence, but can I tell you a secret?" she said. "Your mouth is not your enemy. You might want to listen to the questions and thoughts inside your head and learn to spit them out, just in case."

"In case what?" Cameron managed to ask.

"Right question," she said, "but not one I can answer. Next question?"

"Can you tell me where we're going?"

"To the holding tents."

Holding tents? "What are holding tents?"

"Places we go to torture you."

Cameron smiled.

"It's where we take contestants like you, ones who have the twenty fastest times so far. You'll sit there until either you're out of the top twenty or until we run out of contestants. Meanwhile, our judges will be reviewing tape to make sure there's been no cheating or other funny business. And all you can do is wait. See? Torture."

Cameron's whole body was buzzing even though twenty was far from ten. He took a deep breath, kept putting one foot in front of the other, and concentrated on the heavy concrete structure of the stadium, the fluttering Gollywhopper Games banners, and so many details he'd missed earlier. Good thing they hadn't tested him on finding his way back to the tents. He'd never have made it without a map.

As they entered a smallish room within the tent city, Cameron suddenly detected a puddle on his upper lip, and no doubt his head was sweating buckets.

Sharryn directed him to a chair in the far right corner. Catty-corner was a girl sipping a drink. "What can I get you?" Sharryn asked. "Water? Soda? Juice? Lemonade?"

"Anything wet."

Sharryn disappeared through a tent flap and came back with four cups. "One water, one orange juice, one cola, one lem- onade. All wet." She set them on the table next to him, then draped a hand towel

over his head. She laughed, then waved to the girl. "How're you doing, Clio?"

"I'm still here, right?"

"Yes, you are."

Clio either had found a shower and fresh clothes or had never felt pressure a day in her life. She looked, well, it was stupid, but it was the only word Cameron could think of: She looked crisp. Her cheeks were flushed. Her black hair was silky and straight, no sweat pouring out, and not a strand out of place.

"Do you need anything else?" Sharryn asked her.

"Maybe a bag of chips this time. I've pretty much eaten everything else you have."

"You're not the only one," said Sharryn. She handed Cameron a card. "It's a small menu, but it beats nothing, especially after the long day you've had."

It didn't matter what she brought him. He ordered the first things he saw. "Hot dog and potato chips, please?"

"Catsup? Mustard?"

"Mustard, please."

"You might want Sharryn to bring you a chocolate chip cookie," said Clio. "Best ever."

"And one chocolate chip cookie," said Sharryn. She paused at the tent flap. "Clio already knows this, but you can talk about anything except personal details. No last names, no hometowns, no schools. We don't want you researching each other in case you happen to officially meet tomorrow." She pointed to a camera in another corner of the tent. "It has a sharp microphone."

That sounded ominous. Best to stay silent. He finished his water and started the lemonade.

"Yeah," Clio said. "When I first got here, I was scared to talk about anything, too. But another kid asked me about *stressed* and *hogtie*, and Sharryn okayed that. The kid said he'd been here forever, but a few minutes later some guy beckoned him with a finger, and poof! Disappeared."

"Eliminated?"

"Kinda creepy. Another kid was here for like one minute. Didn't even get her juice before they beckoned, and poof!" Given the circumstances, her laugh might have belonged in a horror movie, but Clio's was a happy, warm, funny laugh.

He made a mental note: Create a laugh video.

He'd have been laughing if he weren't suddenly so wiped. He took the towel off his head. He must look ridiculous. "How long have you been here?"

She motioned around the tent. "No clocks. But long enough to eat a chicken sandwich, a hamburger, some fries, an apple, and two cookies. I get hungry when the pressure's off."

"Me, too."

On cue, Sharryn came through with food. Two hot dogs, two cookies, two bags of chips for Cameron. Chips and an extra cookie for Clio. "This should hold you while I'm gone. I need to send another contestant to the airport. Poor thing doesn't know it yet." She looked at Cameron's cups. "Be back with more water and lemonade."

Cameron allowed himself a small smile. At least for now he was here. "Do you know how long we'll need to wait?"

"Forever," said a Golly person leading in another boy. "We are evil and want to keep you captive as long as possible." He sat the kid in another corner. "P.J., this is Clio and Cameron."

The man in the Golly shirt disappeared behind

the food flap, then leaned back just seconds later with a cup in one hand, beckoning P.J. with the other.

Clio nodded at Cameron, and they waited in silence until P.J. disappeared. "We'll never see him again," she said.

Cameron had to laugh.

"What?"

"You make it sound like he'll vaporize without a trace."

"Maybe he will. We'll never know."

Four more kids came and went. Each time a Golly person beckoned, Cameron's heart deflated, then soared when they didn't kick him out. He and Clio would come to the middle just long enough to high-five. "Survivors!"

"You know," Clio said after the fifth kid had left, "if my best friend, Janae, can't be in here with me— she, of all people, tripped on the obstacle course— I'm glad it's you. You're good at just letting me be."

That might have been the nicest thing Cameron had ever heard. He smiled, then looked away to let her be.

He stretched his arms, his legs. His whole body had tightened the same way it did after his track meets, not that he'd run so much today. Could stress do that?

Clio was lying across three chairs, beating a drummer's cadence on her legs. Maybe that was how she worked out her nerves.

If only he had his videocam to work out his. He'd pan around the tent, then zoom in on little details. Clio's hair swaying off the chair. The drinking straw from his lemonade. Sweat beads on the upper lips of new kids who came in. Once he'd reviewed all the footage, he'd know what to do with it. Just the thought gave him a new sense of calm, but only for a moment.

They had to be near the end. Their plane had landed at 2:02 this afternoon, and when they got to the stadium, the dashboard clock had read 3:08. Hundreds of kids must have finished and headed home before he'd even arrived.

Funny. He'd imagined they'd get to Orchard Heights, check into a hotel, swim, sleep, then compete together in the morning. He'd never pictured sitting here, waiting.

Sharryn strode into the tent. Clio bolted upright. Cameron leaned forward. Who was next to vaporize?

Sharryn beckoned with both hands.

"Nice meeting you," Clio said to Cameron.

"Yeah."

Maybe they'd let him shower before they shoved him back on the plane. There was always the sink in the airport.

"So," said Clio, "is this the vacuum that sucks up the rejects?"

Sharryn shook her head. "No. This is the vacuum that sucks you up and spits you out in a hotel. Four more kids on the course, and none of them will kick either of you out of the top ten."

Clio grabbed him. Or did he grab her? Either way, they were jumping and shouting to the muffled sounds of other kids who'd just received the news in their tents.

"Your drivers and your luggage are waiting for you." Sharryn led them into a central area, where a number of tented hallways spoked off. "Just beyond this point are your families. They only know that you've been on hold. Tell them however you'd like. Cameron, to the left; Clio, to the right."

Balancing his euphoria with Spencer's depression would be tricky. He peered into the tent and caught sight of Spencer sulking in the corner, his parents hovering close, but not too close.

He couldn't help himself. He ran over, and even before he reached them, they knew.

His dad swung him around. "You did it!" he said in a low voice, probably not to rub it into Spencer.

His mom bear-hugged him. "Oh, Cameron!"

Walker came from nowhere and jumped on his back.

For those few brief seconds he was the absolute perfect person in his family's eyes. At least three in his family, anyway.

Cameron eased up to Spencer. "You know you would have had me. I mean, if you hadn't—"

Spencer didn't glare, didn't budge in his chair. He stayed in his hangdog position, bent over at the waist, elbows on knees, head drooping toward the floor. "I flunked the obstacle course. I flunked the freakin' obstacle course." He looked up at Cameron. "You know this is not how things should be."

Cameron nodded. This wasn't the time to disagree with Spencer, but maybe, starting now, this was the way things *could* be.

After the
STADIUM ROUND

Bert Golliwop thought his cheeks might explode the way that one backup generator had. "What happened?"

"An electrical glitch?" said Tawkler from Marketing.

"Electrical glitch, my foot," said Bert. "There were no thunderstorms. There were no reported power surges, says the electric company. Besides, machinery in the off position does not self-destruct."

"At least it didn't affect the integrity of the Games," said Morrison from Legal.

"Not this time," Bert said, "which is the good news. The bad news? We have a rat somewhere among us."

"A rat, sir?" said Jenkins from Human Resources. "Rodents in *this* building, too?"

"Who said anything about rodents?"

"Weren't you talking about the rodent scare at the Kansas arena? I can still feel the gnarled paws of one of those little buggers running over my foot."

"Nobody told me about that," said Bert. "But it doesn't matter. "I'm not talking about that kind of rat. I'm talking about a rat fink, a traitor, a mole."

He hadn't planned on meeting tonight, but he also hadn't imagined that one of tomorrow's puzzles would be all over the Internet. "No one outside the company could have leaked that puzzle."

Bert had to stay rational. He inhaled, exhaled, inhaled. "We've already put an alternate puzzle in place, but that doesn't mean we can rest. We have a traitor living among us." He stared down each member of his leadership team. "Outside of us, there were only ten people privileged to know the puzzles and stunts. The two computers that held that information were fully secured and, I've been told, have not been compromised. The only hard copy is stashed in a safe that has not been opened since I put it there.

"Security has assured me there were no breaches from the outside. From here on out, watch for any unusual activity. Safeguard any delicate information you're working on. Turn your computer screens so they cannot be seen or reflected in the windows behind you. Above all, be my eyes and ears to find out who is doing this to us. Now, go home. Sleep if you can. Tomorrow must go off without a hitch."

CHAPTER 17

This wasn't your typical roadside motel with two squishy beds and one lumpy cot. Golly had given them three adjoining rooms with direct instructions that Cameron have his own. No knees in his back. No fighting for covers. No bathroom wars. And the best—not having to be part of Spencer's pity party.

Cameron could imagine all the other families dancing around and singing at the top of their lungs, which his own family would have been doing if Spencer had made it, too. Or forget "too." If Spencer had made it, period. At least the party in Cameron's head was still popping.

His mom, dad, and brothers were dismantling the

enormous food basket in one room. He was in his, staring into a closet packed with toys and games. For him alone!

His knees buckled. Not from the toys, but because someone had kneed them forward.

Cameron's first instinct was to slam the closet door. Instead, he opened it even wider.

"How do you do that, Walker?"

"Do what?"

"Sneak up on people like that. The army could use you for stealth research."

Walker came around from behind, laughing and shaking muffin crumbs all over the floor. "I saved you the blueberry one." He held it out to Cameron.

"Thanks."

"Whoa!" Walker shoved the rest of the muffin into his mouth. Then he said something that sounded like "Yours?"

Cameron nodded. "Pick something."

"Me?"

"Sure."

Even if Walker chose Mongo-Jongo, the video game Cameron had wanted forever, it didn't matter.

After tomorrow Cameron could buy his own. The losing team members last year had each walked away with one thousand dollars in cash.

Cameron devoured his muffin while Walker pulled out about ten different toys and lined them up. One by one he eliminated a box and put it back in the closet. It got down to Mongo-Jongo and the Zone of Chronos action figure collection.

"Take 'em both," said Cameron.

"No way!" Walker looked up at Cameron, his eyes wide, his mouth in an *O*.

"They're yours."

Walker butt-scooted and grabbed around Cameron's knees to make them buckle again. They rolled on the floor in a wrestling match that had them laughing so hard, they couldn't help but untangle to catch their breath.

Yeah, this was the kind of celebration Cameron was talking about. Even when Spencer marched in, declared that 50 percent belonged to him, and walked away with an armload of stuff from the closet, this was so great!

Not too much later Cameron was staring at the

ceiling from his king-sized bed. The simple thought of the Games should have kept him awake for days, but when his room phone rang, he could barely open his eyes.

He fumbled to pick up the receiver. "Hello?"

"Good morning, Cameron!"

The voice was way too happy for morning.

"It's Sharryn—"

Who?

"—and this is your six-thirty wake-up call. In fifteen minutes room service will knock at your door with breakfast for your family. At eight o'clock sharp, like your instructions said, be downstairs, ready to go. Okay?"

"Uh-huh," he managed to say.

"You're not about to roll over and go back to sleep on me, are you?"

He shook his head.

"If you're shaking your head, Cameron, I can't see you."

Then it hit him. "No, no. I'm awake. Now I'm awake."

She was laughing at the other end when he hung up.

He grabbed his camera and burst into the next room. His dad was already sitting at the edge of the bed, stretching and smiling. The camera caught his mom lifting her head and dropping it back to the pillow.

"They're sending up breakfast," Cameron said. "I hope there's something I like."

"What don't you like?" his dad asked.

"You have a point." Cameron ran to the next room to wake Spencer and Walker, but he stopped short. He didn't need Spencer ragging on him for disrupting his beauty sleep. He backed out of the room and ran to shower.

The clatter of the breakfast carts—a whole buffet on wheels—woke his brothers.

"Did they invite the entire city to eat here?" said his mom.

They didn't need the city. Before Cameron got it all on video, his brothers had already begun to demolish the platters of eggs, pancakes, French toast, and waffles; bowls of fruit and yogurt; plates of bacon, sausage, and steak bites; baskets of rolls, sweet and not; and pitchers of juice, milk, hot chocolate, coffee, and tea.

In the middle was an envelope for Cameron. Spencer reached for it, but even with his camera rolling, Cameron snatched it first.

"Only because I let you," Spencer said.

Who cared if it was the truth? No one was opening Cameron's envelope today. Inside was a plastic packet of lemon juice and a card that said, "Not now. You'll know when."

Spencer grabbed the lemon juice from his hand. "Smart juice? So you can get halfway to intelligent?"

"Spencer," said his dad more sternly than Cameron had ever heard, "it's his day."

"Should've been mine." Spencer put the packet on the table.

Cameron held back a smile. It *was* his day. His dad had said so. He tucked the card and the juice into the pocket of his jeans while he ate. The lemon juice? No question. Reappearing solution for disappearing ink. Would the other kids know? Yeah, or they'd find out. No advantage here.

During the limo ride it was still his day. His parents kept telling him to play smart, try his hardest, and know they were proud of him. Walker kept telling him to kick it. Spencer was unusually silent.

The ten black limos pulled up, parade style, at Golly Headquarters. Cameron's was fifth in line, which, he was told, had no bearing on how he'd finished or on anything to come.

Their driver turned to him. "They're letting you out one at a time, so wait here until I pull up to the red carpet."

"Red carpet?" said Spencer. "He gets to walk the red carpet?"

"You all do," the driver said. Soon he pulled up and opened the doors.

Cameron turned his videocam toward the cheering, sign-waving, camera-clicking spectators flanking the red carpet. At first he suspected Golly had planted all these people to make them feel like big deals. But then he recognized a reporter from one of his mom's Hollywood shows. Was she waiting for someone important? A celebrity's kid or something? Suddenly Cameron had multiple microphones thrust at him.

"What's your name? How old are you? Where are you from? What's with the video camera? How surprised are you to be a finalist? Are those your brothers? Ooh. The tall one's cute. Can I have your autograph? Can I have his?"

With Golly people surrounding them and shuttling them into the doors, though, Cameron was barely able to say his name. "Who do you think they're waiting for?" he asked Spencer.

"Seriously? Don't you know you guys are stars now? And that I will forever be known as Cameron's brother?"

Cameron smiled inside. "Welcome to my world," he said under his breath.

"What?"

"Nothing."

Spencer pinched his arm. "What?"

"Nothing. We're nothings right now. We haven't done anything."

"You don't get it. You have the chance to be the next Gil. Or the boy version of Bianca. Well, not her. You'd need more personality and looks, but people all over the world will know your name."

Poor Spencer. He would have loved the attention, the fame, and adoring fans.

Not Cameron. He needed to forget about being in any spotlight; otherwise, he'd forever be known as the kid who sat babbling in a puddle of his own drool. It had been bad enough at that spelling bee. He'd been able to spell "succumb" in his sleep until he got onstage in front of two hundred people. And now it wouldn't be two hundred people watching him; it'd be zillions.

Sharryn met them at the door. "Great to see you all again! At least for a little while. In a few minutes, Cameron, I will turn you over to a couple of familiar faces. Bill and Carol will be your guides from here on out."

On the rare occasions Cameron had allowed himself to dream about getting this far, Bill and Carol had been part of the fantasy. For the last year, people at school and online had debated which guide they'd rather have. Cameron didn't care. They both gave the same information and cheered on their teams equally. The difference was in their styles. Carol put an arm around her kicked-out people, then gently sent them to their families. When Bill's team was eliminated, he gathered them in a huddle, then gave the best pep talk Cameron had ever heard: They'd each been one of ten people in the whole world who had made it this far; on any other day they'd be the ones continuing on; they needed to hold their heads high and be proud. Maybe it wasn't original, but coming from Bill, it would have Cameron ready to conquer the world.

Sharryn led his family to a small conference room, where his parents signed even more forms. And before he'd shot barely two minutes of good footage, Sharryn herded Cameron out the door and down the hall. "Here we go."

Cameron panned the pictures on the walls—pictures of stern-looking men and women with wacky props. Water was squirting from one guy's ears. One woman had a pair of skunks on her head. Another had a daisy mustache.

"Team competition time," said Sharryn. "Excited?"

Cameron was focused on the picture of the man with a snake smiling through tufts of his hair. He nodded.

"Nervous?" said Sharryn.

Cameron nodded again.

"And the camera helps?"

Cameron smiled at her.

"You know," she said, putting a hand on his camera hand, "it'll help your nerves if you don't bottle everything up. So tell me how it feels to be excited."

Cameron lowered the camera. "It's like I have this lava pool that's starting at my knees and bubbling around my stomach. But it's more warm than hot, and I'm still not sure if it's giving me energy or getting me ready to throw up."

"Let's hope for energy," said Sharryn, "but let me know if it's the other. We can stop at a bathroom along the way. In fact—"

She stopped and pointed down a hall. "Third door on the right. Bathroom. Go splash some water on your face, and take a few deep breaths. I'll hold on to your camera so it doesn't get wet. And I promise nothing will happen to it. Sound good?"

It did.

"Take your time," she said. "The Games can't start without you."

He closed himself into a stall and leaned against the door to breathe. This might be the only moment of the day he couldn't mess up. In less than an hour Bill or Carol might be sending him to the losers' room. Then, in a few weeks, he'd have to explain to the kids at school how he wasn't quite good enough. As usual.

There was only one antidote for that: winning the whole thing. But how would that even be possible? How had he gotten this far? What exactly had he done? Nothing extraordinary, really. He'd just tried his hardest.

Cameron came out of the stall, washed his hands, and splashed some water on his face. Is that all he needed to do? Try his hardest? Support his team? His team. This next part wasn't all on his shoulders!

He splashed more water on his face. What if his team discovered that he wasn't special, that he was as bogus as a green-striped zebra, as phony as a thirteen-hour clock, as fake as a cinnamon-scented cabbage? Wasn't a chain only as strong as its weakest link? What if he was the weakest?

Even this private pep talk was a disaster. He diverted some water into his mouth, swished it around, and spit it out. He grabbed a bunch of paper towels, wiped his hands, then held them against his face. He was panicking the way Spencer did with word problems. He had to treat this like math. One step at a time. He could follow directions. He could unravel questions. He could reason things out. He'd done better than Spencer, who could do anything. He could do this. *I can do this,* he mouthed. "I can do this," he whispered. "I can do this," he said.

Cameron pushed open the door to an empty hallway and walked toward the spot where Sharryn had left him. No Sharryn. Maybe he'd turned the wrong way. He went back past the bathroom and to an open office. Maybe Sharryn was in there.

Cameron peeked in and saw heaven. The large room was loaded with monitors, lots of them. All the screens sat above banks and banks of buttons and levers and switches. A TV control center? The hub of busyness once all the cameras were rolling? Could Cameron just stay here? Well, not today. On any normal day he'd have been more than satisfied to watch the producers decide which camera angles to use and how to edit this together. But today he had the chance to do something he'd never be able to do ever again.

Still, he could take a few more seconds in here. He counted sixteen monitors, all dark except for three larger ones in the center, each showing the same picture of fireworks, ones he hoped would go off for him at the end.

This felt good. This felt natural. This is what he wanted to do with his life. No matter if he was first to get kicked out, made a total fool of himself on national TV, or otherwise messed up, it wouldn't need to permanently mark him, not when there was the rest of his life and a world full of cameras to use.

He backed out of the room, walked a few doors down, the wrong way. He retraced his steps and waited near the bathroom for Sharryn and whatever the Games would hand him.

Cameron was ready. He could do this.

CHAPTER 18

Sharryn rounded the corner just seconds later. "I hope I didn't keep you waiting."

He shook his head. He almost asked her about the TV room but didn't want to get in trouble for wandering.

"You certainly look different. Throw up?"

"No," said Cameron. "I decided I can do this."

"Of course you can." She handed him his videocam and led him back the way they'd come. "If you couldn't, you wouldn't be here. Our challenges are designed to weed out people who can't do this."

"Really?"

"Really. And how does that make you feel?"

"Even better."

"Then my job here is done." Sharryn stopped at a door. "Your journey continues inside." She squeezed his shoulder. "It was a pleasure, Cameron. You can do this."

He smiled and held up his camera. "Can I record that?"

"Of course." She planted her feet and looked straight into the lens. "You can do this, Cameron. And even better, you finally know you can. Now, go in there."

Cameron kept recording, his hand turning the doorknob, the vestibule inside, the blue door and the orange door opposite him, the faces. Faces? The guides!

"Cameron!" said Carol.

"Welcome!" said Bill. "Whose team do you want to be on? Mine or hers?"

Cameron held the videocam as a barrier between him and his answer. Did he really have to—

"No doubt," said Bill. "He wins for the most alarmed reaction so far."

Carol put a little pressure on Cameron's arm. He

lowered the camera. "You don't have to choose," she said. "Not that way."

Cameron breathed.

"It's the luck of the draw," said Bill. He held up a large wooden block with three jester heads sticking out. There was also one hole where apparently a jester used to be.

"Here's the drill," said Bill. "Boys pick from my block; girls, from hers."

Carol's block had four jesters remaining. "If your jester's wearing an orange shirt, you're on the Orange Team with me."

"And if your jester's wearing a blue shirt, you're with me on the Blue Team," said Bill. "Choose wisely."

Cameron's hand hovered over the jester in the far corner; then he grabbed one in front.

"Oh, yeah," said Bill. "I have my first boy!" He opened the blue door for Cameron. "Go ahead in. I'll be with you in a few."

Inside the blue door and above a large table was a ceiling full of balloons, and around him were walls with fun-house mirrors and giant toys.

A girl with bouncy reddish blond hair stood behind a chair. She carried herself like she planned to be the next Bianca, except her eyes weren't as, um, well, he didn't know what the right word was. They actually looked a little mean. "Who are you?" she said to Cameron. "Kid or camera crew?"

"Kid," said Cameron.

"And what's this on your camera?"

Cameron felt his head start to sweat. "Bianca signed it."

"*The* Bianca?" said the girl. "Seriously? I so want to be her. I'm Dacey, by the way." She looked him up and down. "And you are . . ."

"Sorry. I'm Cameron."

"Well, if that's not cute as all get out—Cameron with the camera." Maybe it was supposed to sound "cute," but her tone matched her eyes. "How'd that happen?"

Cameron ran his free hand over a chair back. He wanted to shrug and keep filming, but he needed to start this team thing off right. "When I was born, my grandmother misheard my dad, thought he'd said my name was Camera. I mean, who names a kid Camera?"

"My middle name is Table."

Oops. A girl with a ponytail had come through the door.

"Just kidding," she said. "I'm Estella. And behind me is Clio."

Clio came in with a big smile. It was good to see her.

But Dacey was staring them down, especially Estella, as if they'd done something to ruin her party. Then Dacey stepped closer to Cameron and gave him a fake grin. "So, cute little Cameron here was explaining why his name matches what appears to be his third arm."

Just when he thought he'd escaped Spencer's sarcasm, *she* had to show up.

"I think it's cool," said Estella. "Finish your story."

Cameron tried not to breathe an

audible sigh of relief. "That day my grandmother bought me a camera to remember her mistake. I started using it, my mom says, before my second birthday, and I've pretty much had a camera in my hand ever since."

"So they're lettin' you film this whole thing?" asked Dacey.

"Doubtful." But he had his camera now and focused on the door as it opened.

America's alternate, Jig Jiggerson, swaggered in and almost seemed to pose. He still had the great smile he'd flashed at the camera no matter how frustrated he must have been on the sidelines last year.

Almost on Jig's heels, Bill came bounding into the room. He pretended to sneak up on the life-sized polar bear; then he turned it around, unzipped its back, reached in, and pulled out five blue Gollywhopper Games T-shirts. He threw one at each of them. "These should be your sizes. If you prefer to change in the bathroom, we can arrange it."

"Excuse me," said Dacey, her nose sort of twitching. "But do we need to wear this? I mean, my mama and I shopped for days to find the right outfit. And this color blue clashes with the blue in my jeans."

"No," said Bill. "You don't have to wear it. We can always get the first alternate in here."

"Maybe they should," Estella whispered.

Dacey didn't seem to hear. "Fine," she said. "Bathroom?"

Cameron and Jig changed in the room. Then Cameron sat at the table and filmed Jig punching a bounce-back alien until Bill and the girls returned.

"I've told a certain young woman who's unhappy with the wardrobe," said Bill, "that a certain camera most likely captured her in all her fashionable glory. If she agrees, Cameron, might you post that later for the world to see?"

"Sure."

"But for now . . ." Bill reached for the videocam.

Cameron paused, then handed it over.

"Ooh, that face," Bill said. "Don't worry, my man. We won't lose it. Promise."

"Thanks," he said.

"Dacey, Jig. Cell phones, please."

They handed them over.

"Don't worry, Dacey. It'll be safe with your clothes

and your purse. And now I believe," said Bill, "that's all for your electronics, right?"

Dacey reached to her waist and took off a little black box. "Pedometer," she said. "I'm workin' on one million steps before school starts. Can I—"

Bill shook his head. "Sorry. Anyone else before our detectors embarrass you?"

Jig gave a low whistle. "Man, you are strict this year!"

"We are," said Bill. "And you especially should appreciate that. Our alternates are waiting for any of you to make that one fatal error. Now, have a seat around the table."

Each of them grabbed a seat, fast.

"Ha!" said Bill. "Threats work. So fifty lashes or danger of being disqualified if you don't listen to these instructions. Ready?"

They nodded. So did Bill.

A monitor showing Carol came down from the ceiling. "To ensure you receive the instructions in the same way," she said, "you get us both. Our team has me in the room and you on the screen, Bill."

"My team likewise, except you on-screen," said

Bill. "Now, in a few minutes we will send each team to identical but separate Golly warehouse rooms like the ones you probably saw on TV last year."

High fives went all around.

"Once you're there," Carol said, "you'll go through a puzzle-stunt sequence with a twist or two thrown in. To start, you'll find an envelope with your first puzzle. The answer to that puzzle will be represented by one of three Golly products. And those will be conveniently located on a nearby table. Each choice table will also hold pens and paper to use however you need. With us so far?"

They were.

"Okay," said Bill. "When and only when you've decided on the correct answer, open the corresponding product. Inside will be directions for a stunt. If you perform the stunt correctly, you will receive a new puzzle. If you opened the wrong Golly product, it will have you perform the wrong stunt, and you will receive the puzzle you thought you'd already solved."

"Oh, and we're so generous here," said Carol. "We will generously add a five-minute penalty to your score on top of the time you wasted doing it all wrong."

"The reason for that—"

Dacey raised her hand.

"Yes, Dacey?" said Bill.

"I want to tell you the reason."

Ehhh! Bill's buzzer impersonation was perfect. "I'm sure you do, Dacey, but we have to be the ones to tell you. And I can tell you, we threaten to shower you with penalties to ensure that you work at solving each puzzle. We have the whole place wired for sound and picture. We're like Santa Claus. We know what you're doing every single millisecond. Not only will you get a five-minute penalty for opening the wrong package, but you'll get an additional twenty-minute penalty if you open any product without having a logical reason."

"It all boils down to this," said Carol. "The team with the fastest time advances to the next round."

"We will be lurking in the shadows if you need us—first-aid kits, bathroom passes, hoorays and huzzahs, and all that jazz. But outside of telling you where you stand in comparison to the other team, you're strictly on your own."

"We wish we could help you," said Carol. "Or I wish I could help *my* team, because Bill and I have another side bet this year."

Bill rubbed his hand over his short hair. "It grew back after Carol graciously shaved it for me, but I'd have little to lose if we kept the same bet this time."

"Instead, the bet is maid service," Carol explained. "Once a week for a year. Either he comes to my house to clean or I come to his. So Orange Team, do for me what Green did last year. Win!"

"Or not," said Bill. "Her house, I understand, is a pigsty."

"And his, I understand, puts the term 'pigsty' to shame. So there you have it," Carol said. "Work hard for us. Oh, please, Orange Team, work hard for me, but more important, work hard for yourselves, play hard for yourselves, and above all, have fun."

"And this ends our joint instructional session," said Bill. "See you, Orange Team."

"See you, Blue!" Carol said.

The screen went blank, then rose back into the ceiling.

Bill thrust a bunch of papers into the air. "And

now, for your reading pleasure, written instructions." He handed a stapled set to each of them. "It's what we just said, but in official language. So read. Absorb. Sign. When you're all done, talk. Get acquainted. Then we'll get these Games started." He left the room.

Cameron somehow found the attention to read the rules. As Bill had said, nothing different, except maybe more about cheating. Cameron signed his and sat back.

Clio was already finished, then Dacey, then Jig. Estella kept reading, though. If she was that slow on everything, she could be a problem.

Dacey looked annoyed. She sighed once and again.

Finally Estella signed. Cameron waited for Dacey to ask what had taken so long, but thankfully she didn't. There was already enough friction bristling in the air.

Dacey did lean forward from the head of the table and point to Cameron. "So we know you're Cameron with the camera. And Clio, like Cleopatra, has long dark hair. Everyone remembers Jig Jiggerson from last year. I'm Dacey Dahlgren, but don't let this southern accent and strawberry blond hair make you think of me as all lacy. I can be tough. And you?" She pointed toward Estella. "I'm sorry, but I don't think we truly met."

"I'm the one you sighed at while I was trying to understand exactly what I was signing. You just don't sign things without reading them. You could get into trouble."

"Thank you, but what's your name?"

"Estella Serio."

"I'm sorry," said Dacey. "Can you say your first name again?"

"Eh-stay-uh," Estella enunciated.

"Eh-stay-uh?"

"Exactly."

"I'm sorry again," said Dacey. "I'm just havin' a hard time visualizing that. Can you spell it for me?"

"What is this?" said Estella. "National Spelling Bee? E-S-T-E-L-L-A."

Jig laughed. "She's a magician. She made the *L*'s disappear."

"Why do you people do that with your language?" said Dacey. "Why don't you pronounce all the letters the right way?

"You mean, like in English with 'comb' and 'laughter'?" Estella said.

Dacey laughed. "But then there's that other thing. Why in the middle of talking normal do you do that thing with your *R*'s? Ser-r-rio."

"Because that's my name."

"Dear me," said Dacey, "I didn't mean to be rude. It's just my nerves all actin' up. You should see me backstage at my pageants. Woo-boy!"

Jig sat back and chuckled. "So you're a beauty queen, Dacey. Figures."

"Was a beauty queen," said Dacey. "As in past tense. As in movin' on. As in shakin' free of that dumb Laura Ramirez, who the judges love so much. More than money, I think. Not that we tried to bribe them, but they liked her more than something everyone should like."

"Like you?" Estella asked.

"Exactly. And not just that, but there's more to life than worryin' about your makeup every single second."

Cameron stifled a smile. He'd never seen so much makeup on one face in his life.

Estella shook her head. "You're not too smart, are you?"

"I was smart enough to pay attention to the stadium study guide, and it got me here, didn't it?"

"You mean Gil's stuff?" said Jig.

"Whatever. I mean, I decided it's time to promote my brains more than my pageant wave." She raised her hand and swiveled it side to side in the most fake greeting Cameron had ever seen.

"Why do you need to promote anything?" asked Estella.

"The more people notice the positives in you, the more opportunity you have for success. Isn't that just a fact of the world?"

Estella shook her head. "Not my world."

"What's your world then?"

"No, lacy Dacey. I don't know you well enough."

"Oh, *pshaw*," said Dacey. "You can get a little more personal."

Estella's eyes narrowed, but Clio cleared her throat. "I'd like to hear more, Estella."

"You seem nice, Clio," Estella said. "So, fine. In my world we don't have time to brag. My parents work three jobs, hoping they can put me and my little brother and sister through college. So I cook a lot and babysit and supervise homework."

"You gonna supervise us?" asked Jig.

Estella shook her head. "This is like a vacation for me."

"You mean like lazin' back and sippin' umbrella drinks?" said Dacey.

Estella laughed. "Sure. Why not?"

"Fabulous." Dacey shifted her whole body away from Estella and fully focused on Cameron.

Uh-oh.

"So you're Cameron. Did I know your last name?"

"Schein."

"Like 'rise and shine'?" Dacey lit up with her smile.

Cameron couldn't help but smile back. "Spelled differently, but yeah."

"Mine, too!" said Clio. "My last name sounds like a real word, too."

"What word?" said Jig.

"True, as in 'true or false,'" said Clio, "but the *U* and the *E* are transposed."

"What's that mean?" Dacey asked.

"Switched around. Spelled T-R-E-U."

Dacey looked at Clio like she was going to challenge her with some question, but instead, she turned toward Jig. "I just have to get this out of the way," she said, "but Jig, that's not your real name, or is it?"

"It's what everyone calls me, so it's about as real as a name gets."

"No, silly," said Dacey. "That's not what's on your birth certificate, is it?"

"*Ding, ding, ding!* Give her a prize." Jig stood and stretched probably close to six feet tall. "If you have those brains you speak of, you'll call me Jig. Just Jig." He winked at her.

Her smile glowed. "I get you."

Cameron didn't get it at all. Was he too young to understand? He was twelve. Estella was thirteen. Clio and Dacey were fourteen, and Jig was fifteen. He was, however, old enough to know that Dacey and Jig and Estella were competing with everyone already.

When Bill had said they should get acquainted, Cameron had assumed it would be, "Hi. I'm Cameron, I'm twelve years old, but I'll be thirteen in two months. I'm pretty good at math, so I hope there will be some math coming up. And yeah, that's about it."

But no. Besides knowing each one's name and age, the only thing Cameron truly learned was to stay away from Dacey. No way he wanted to tangle with her.

CHAPTER 19

Bill came back in. "Here we go!"

They walked through three halls, down two floors, through a body scanner and found themselves in a tree- and bird-populated atrium with two massive doors looming ahead, one orange, one blue.

"Behind these doors?" Bill said. "Ten times more spectacular than on TV. When you go inside, your jaws will drop and your eyes will bug out. I suggest wiggling your fingers in your line of sight to snap yourself back to reality; then sprint to that first puzzle envelope on the blue-lit table in front of you. Think hard, team. Play smart. I hate to clean houses."

The Orange Team poured into the atrium.

Bill stared at Carol. Carol stared at Bill. They both put on headsets and lowered their microphones toward their lips.

"Any last words to your troops?" he said.

"We've already had our little talk. Let's do this."

And with that, the two-story doors swung open on their own.

A voice came from nowhere. "Time starts . . . *now!*"

Two steps in. That was all it took for Cameron to stop dead in his tracks. He'd never exactly seen a snow-capped mountain inside a building. But there it was in the distance. Closer to him, a clock with enormous multicolored gears, a giant pineapple, a speedboat, a golden shaft of light, jack-o'-lanterns, real lanterns, peacocks, cowboy hats, and layered birthday cakes with sparkler candles. And that was at first glance.

Bill was right. Cameron waved his fingers in front of his eyes to snap out of his instant trance. They couldn't waste time. He sped four steps diagonally to the blue-lit table with an envelope marked "Puzzle #1." No one followed. Time to use his voice. "Um," he said.

Clio moved her eyes toward him. "Hey!" she said. "Cameron has the envelope."

They gathered around him.

"Open it already," said Dacey.

He did and pulled out a card.

Puzzle #1

* * * * * * * * * *

Ja	Nie
Da	Tidak
Jah	Nein
Po	Ne
Sí	No
Yes	Yok
Ja	Nej

(Your choices are underneath the table.)

Cameron had already decided that the words said "yes" or "no" in different languages even before Jig pulled up three Golly games: Agree to Disagree, Jupiter Fighter, Greased Piglets.

"Time to work," said Estella. Then she and Jig and Dacey started talking over one another fast and loud as if speed and volume would win them something.

"Hush, y'all!" Dacey won the battle of the voices. "The yes-no thing is obvious."

"She's right," Estella said. "We'll get nowhere like this. We need some order."

"If you have any ideas outside the obvious," said Jig, "say them. That's how the Green Team won last year, brainstorming." Jig smacked the puzzle card onto the table.

They stood around it, staring. With all those yeses and nos, Agree to Disagree was the most obvious choice, but last year's puzzles had never worked that way. They basically spelled out the answer. Here, seven yeses and seven nos. Two of the games each had two seven-letter words in their names. His turn to talk. "There's—"

"With the yes-no thing," Jig said, cutting him off, "it's gonna be one of the first two."

"Yeah," said Dacey. "I'll just die if I have to rustle up a bunch of greased pigs."

Cameron hadn't gotten this far to let them railroad him into the wrong answer, but it was useless to talk over these guys. He rattled Agree to Disagree, but it didn't get their attention.

Clio, though, stepped to the other side of the table. "You're looking at this wrong." She nodded at Jig. "If *you* watched last year, you'll remember each puzzle pretty much spelled out the name of a toy or game. And here we have fourteen yeses and nos altogether. Fourteen letters in the names of the last two games."

Estella smiled. "So if all the yeses relate to letters in the first word of the correct game and all the nos relate to letters in the second word, then we've got it."

Thank you, Clio and Estella.

"I've got it, y'all!" said Dacey.

They turned to her like she was the only bottle of water in the Sahara.

"Well, I don't have *it*. I was going to say that maybe the first or last letters of each yes or no spelled something—"

"But they don't," said Estella, finishing Dacey's sentence.

Dacey shot her a look.

Those two were like oil and water. Or maybe baking soda and vinegar, the stuff fake lava is made of. Cameron couldn't control them, but if they messed up, he'd have an excuse for losing. Or not. He'd blame himself for not stepping in.

Right now, they were off track. It wasn't the

words themselves that mattered. One column meant yes; the other, no. "It's not the words." He whispered to hear himself. "It's the languages. Why did they choose those languages in that order? The names of the languages could spell—"

Clio touched him on the shoulder. "You're right," she said to Cameron. Then she turned to the others. "You all need to hear this."

They looked at Clio. She glanced at Cameron, but the rest were still looking at her. She shrugged and started talking. "If you match the words with the languages they come from, maybe the first initials of those languages spell out the right game."

"Do you speak all these languages?" said Dacey. "I don't speak all these languages."

"You don't have to," said Clio. "We can start with the ones we know. Like yes. English is the only language that officially uses 'yes.' So if the sixth letter in the first word is an *E* for 'English,' then—"

"Well, isn't that the perfect example?" said Dacey. "The *E* works for 'Greased' and 'Jupiter.'"

Cameron tried to shut out her nastiness and focus on another word. Wasn't *nein* German for "no"? And the third letter in "Piglets" was *G*! But it was also the third in "Fighter."

"What about *sí*? That's 'yes' in Spanish, and it's—"

"Well, whoopie, Estella!" said Dacey. "You take Spanish, too."

Estella shook her head. "*Yo no tomo español, hablo español todos los días. No importa.* Never mind."

Jig shook his head. "What'd she say?"

Dacey shrugged.

Jig wouldn't let it go. "Estella. What'd you say?"

"Stop wasting time. Focus on the puzzle."

"That's not what you said."

"Of course it's not what I said. Do you really care or do you want to win?"

Now both Dacey and Jig were glaring at her. It was worse than having Spencer around.

"I was going to say," said Estella, "that *si* is also 'yes' in Italian, but I don't know if the Italian *si* has the same accent. Also that *ja* must mean 'yes' in two different languages because neither of the first words starts and ends with the same letter. That plus *N-O* means 'no,' as you should know, Jig, in English, Spanish, Italian, and probably some others."

"Really?" said Clio. "I didn't know that. What about any of these? Do you know more of these, Estella? Anyone?"

Cameron knew *da*—his friend Max's great-grandfather was from Russia—but if *da* was also "yes" in a *U* language, they couldn't eliminate Jupiter Fighter, and he didn't want Jig or someone to jump the gun and open Greased Piglets, then blame him if he was wrong.

"What's *yok*?" said Jig. "Something you scramble? Something you hook to an ox?"

"Seriously?" said Estella. "Be serious."

Enough. Cameron dropped to his knees and crawled under the blue-lit table.

"Look," said Jig. "That's him being serious. You groveling?"

"No," Cameron said. "Looking to see if they taped a translation guide to the underside."

"Did they?"

"No."

Jig laughed. "Or *nie*, *tidak*, *nein*—"

"Wait," said Clio. "Did I hear you say something about *nein*, Cameron?"

"It's German, but the third letter is *G* in both second words."

"At least we're on the right track. Oh! I have an idea. Look at it backwards."

"You mean, 'rethgif retipuj'? 'Stelgip desaerg'?" Dacey laughed at her pathetic joke.

"No," Clio said. "If you take the *F* in 'Fighter,' for example, the top word of column two would need to be in an *F* language. Like *N-O-N* in French. Not *N-I-E* in—" Clio let out a sigh of frustration. "As far as I know, *N-I-E* could be Finnish."

"We need a translation guide," said Dacey. "Oh! Y'all! Maybe they have books in our conference room!" She and Jig turned to run, but that was a waste.

"No!" Cameron stopped them in their tracks. "I specifically noticed there weren't." While he had their attention, he kept going. "But I might know another word."

"Whatcha been waiting for?" said Dacey.

He tried to ignore her tone. "*Da* is Russian for 'yes.'"

"Only one of them has an *R* in that position," said Estella. "Are you sure?"

"I'm sure."

"Why didn't you tell us in the first place?" said Jig.

"If there's a *U* language, it could be 'Jupiter Fighter,' too."

"Does a *U* language exist?" asked Jig. He picked up Greased Piglets. "We tried to reason this out so they can't penalize us. Anyone object?"

"Only if it gets us all greasy," said Dacey.

While Jig opened the box, Estella leaned over to Cameron, "Good job."

"Good job," echoed Clio.

Cameron hoped it was a good job, or they'd be all over him.

Jig pulled out their stunt card.

STUNT #1
＊＊＊＊＊＊＊＊＊＊

Our pigs are on unplanned release.
What's worse, they've tracked through
pools of grease!
Go find the greasy pigs and then
move all of them from field to pen.
Two rules:
1. You each must place two pigs exactly
where we ask.

**2. You each must wear our special gloves
to carry out this task.
Oink!**

"Thank heaven they have gloves for us," said Dacey.

"But where are they?" said Jig. "There were arrows last year." He turned toward the entrance. "Yoo-hoo! Bill! Where are the pigs?"

Silence.

"Yo, Bill!"

Nothing.

"Then it's a warehouse search!" Jig zoomed toward the rear of the massive room. Why there? Why not to the right or the left or somewhere near the first clue? How could he know where to go?

Still, they followed him like Mary's little lambs. At worst, they were getting a good overview of what they might need later. They passed a beach of sea turtles, tubas, tuba-sized ice skates, giant stuffed aliens, a zebra-headed candy cane, a towering vase sprouting ceiling-high flowers, a wall of boomerangs, a kitchen, an oil derrick, and a rack of Shooter

String before they got to the back of the warehouse. But no pigs.

"At least we know where they aren't," said Dacey.

"And don't you go taking off again." Estella sounded like a scolding mom.

"Bill didn't say anything about sticking together," Clio said. "We'll cover more ground if we split up in different directions."

Estella sectioned off the warehouse, assigning Cameron the front right. It made sense to focus forward and speed to his area, but it wouldn't hurt to mentally map the place. Once he'd cataloged the elephant bath, the neon orange forklift, the sunflower field, the green wall, and the blinking banks of lights, he pretty much gave up memorizing his path. In fact, he'd veered off course. Where was he? Why didn't this place come with a GPS? He stopped and looked toward the ceiling, looked to find a corner to the right. There! Cameron was almost to his area when one of the girls shouted, "Here! Here!"

The "here" came from behind him and to the left.

"Where's here?" yelled Jig.

"Look up. Cow! Moon!" said the voice.

Way in back, a cow was jumping over the moon, turning, and jumping again. Cameron kept his focus upward and raced as quickly as his legs would carry him.

Dacey pulled up right behind him. "No-o-o!"

"Heh-heh," said Jig. "Your worst nightmare."

The fenced-in field, about the size of Cameron's school's band room, looked mucky and slick. So did the ten motorized pigs running around inside. Cameron leaned through the fence to touch the ground. "It's not muddy."

"It's not?" Dacey asked.

He stood. "The ground only looks muddy. It's ridged, but it's hard."

"Which isn't getting us anywhere." Estella pointed to the far side of the fence. "Gloves, I think."

The gloves were more like socks. No place for fingers. No place for thumbs.

"This is so gross," said Dacey.

She was right. The outsides of the "gloves" were greasy, and the insides were just as slimy, as if they'd been soaking in oil overnight. The pigs were shiny, too. They almost looked real, about a foot and a half long, their heads about that same distance from the ground. They were rigged to dart around fast. Not only that, but they were quaking and shaking and sort of heaving as they moved.

Jig hurdled the four-foot fence, caught up with a pig, and reached down several inches in front like he was anticipating it moving into his hands. The pig veered away as if it had radar.

"Let me show you how," said Dacey. "Unfortunately, I've been privileged to do this before. More than once. Word to the wise: Don't enter the Miss Ragin' Razorback contest." She ran up to a pig, lowered her hands, and her sock gloves slid off.

"Wedge them between your fingers from the back side." Clio grabbed Dacey's hand. "Like this."

"Thanks." She gave Clio a smile that almost looked genuine. "Okay. So now you stand straddle-legged, reach down, and stab at them." She did, but the pig was out of there before she clapped her hands together.

"Thanks for the lesson," said Jig. "Just go for it, everyone."

Cameron targeted a pig. He reached toward its

nose with one hand and its tail with the other, but he lost it before he got traction. The little sucker accelerated away. There had to be Golly people with remote controls making this impossible. No one had even come close.

"Hey!" said Estella. "Listen to my idea."

Cameron straightened for a second to stretch his back.

"These piggies can't run wild if there's no place for them to run. We need to corner them. That corner over there." She pointed to the right.

They gathered in a *C* and tried to herd the pigs to the opposite corner, but a few sidestepped them and scooted behind.

"It won't work if we don't have them all," said Estella. "The others will just run loose."

"Where's she going?" said Dacey.

Clio had thrown off her gloves, had climbed the fence, and was coming back with a large camel. She handed it to Jig. "I don't think they can climb. We need to barricade them into a corner."

Jig set the camel upright, but Clio laid it on its side, turning it into a wall.

They each climbed the fence and came back with an object. They added a stoplight, stoplight-sized hot dog, jack-in-the-box, foot, and cheese wedge. Then they worked together, moving the wall of objects forward and shoving the pigs to a corner. The pigs were still shuddering and moving, but they were also bumping into one another.

"Enough," said Clio. "We need room for ourselves."

There was enough room for two. Dacey and Jig went first. What should have been easy still wasn't. The wiggling pigs kept slipping from their greasy gloves.

"If only I didn't need to keep my fingers clenched together," said Dacey.

"Just clench a couple of them," said Clio.

And maybe if they grabbed smaller parts—

Cameron needed to say that out loud. "The pigs aren't real. Grab the ears; you can't hurt them."

"Yeah! Did you hear that?" Clio said much louder.

"Hear what?" said Jig.

"Grab their ears or their feet. Nothing against that in the rules."

Jig got a hand on an ear and a foot, but why'd he let it go? Maybe he didn't. The pig was wriggling and shaking. He held on the second time. "Where does this thing go?"

"Right in front of you," said Estella.

Just outside the field was the pigpen, a giant, hollowed-out, writing type of pen all decked out with pictures of pigs and, more important, with ten compartments. Jig leaned over the fence and shoved his pig into one of them. The pig shut down.

"That's one," said Clio.

"Two!" Dacey said.

In quick succession they each got their second pigs. Now there was enough room for the other three to get in.

Cameron butt-slid over the camel and came toe-to-toe with a pig. It darted to his right but bumped into Estella's leg. "Hold still, Estella." She did, and he grabbed an ear and a leg like he'd seen Jig do. "Five!"

"Six!" said Clio. And about ten seconds later: "Seven!"

Again there was too much space. The remaining three pigs were darting around again.

"Either move in the hot dog and foot or come help us corner these," Estella said.

Jig barely nudged the hot dog. Clio and Dacey climbed the fence to help.

Cameron didn't want to lose the pig he almost had. He charged at it with one leg and somehow knocked it on its side. Its wheels were spinning, and its body was wriggling; but it was going nowhere. He picked it up. "Eight!"

"What's the deal, Estella?" said Dacey. "Get a pig already."

"You're doing fine," said Clio. "Try what Cameron did. Try to knock one on its side. Kick it if you want. It's not alive."

"But they look so alive," said Estella. "All wriggly and pink like newborns."

"They're mechanical pigs," said Jig. "Get over it."

Cameron stepped next to her and herded the pig a little closer to the corner. Clio joined him, and within a minute Estella had numbers nine and ten in the pen.

Puzzle time! But nothing happened.

"Bill! Where's the envelope?" yelled Jig.

"Yeah," said Dacey. "I swear, Cameron, if you were wrong about—"

"Stop it!" said Clio. "Maybe it's the numbers on their bellies."

"What numbers?" said Dacey.

"See?" said Clio. "The first one has a five. The next one has an eight." She picked both up. "We should each move two of them in case that's part of the rules."

They took out all the pigs and replaced them, one at a time, in numerical order.

"Here goes number ten," said Estella. She slid in the last pig, and a wide banner unfurled from a beam that seemed suspended in midair.

Cameron's heart raced. *Please don't say Puzzle #1.* He couldn't bear the blame if he'd failed them.

CHAPTER 20

"We did it!" Dacey and Jig high-fived as if they had made this happen by themselves.

Spanning the width of the banner were eight pictures: a nest, microscope, chicken coop with one rooster inside, empty egg carton, cup and saucer, sleeve, hayloft, and a bumpy, green thing. Underneath it read "PUZZLE #2."

Bill appeared from behind the banner, throwing towels so they could clean up. "Brilliant use of resources," he said. "But you're neck and neck with the other team. Go!" And he slid back around.

Jig pointed to the banner. "Our puzzle, I presume."

"That's it?" said Dacey. "Just pictures?"

"Obviously," said Estella.

Dacey waved a hand in the air. "Ooh! I've got it. It's one of those picture puzzles!"

"Well, duh," said Jig.

"No," she said. "Those rebuses. Like a picture of a skirt, then a minus sign, then the letter *S*, then a plus sign, then a map of the Mediterranean, which would equal 'curtsy.'"

"Where'd you come up with that one?" said Jig. "Curtsy. Ha!"

"Well, pardon my third-grade teacher," Dacey said.

Estella shook her head. "So that's what fills your brain. Rebuses from third grade."

Okay then. No way Cameron would admit to learning in first grade that the Brazilian gold frog is the size of a dime.

"Sorry," said Clio, "but does that really matter?"

"It doesn't," Estella said, "because the puzzle is not a rebus."

Dacey put a hand on her hip. "Why not?"

"Where are the minuses? Where are the pluses?"

"Where are the choices?" Clio said.

Cameron pointed to the banner. Very small, in the bottom-right corner, almost fading into the fabric, was an arrow at the end of a line that trailed right, then looped back onto itself.

The choices were on a table behind the banner. Had it been there before? Didn't matter. They had choices! JinxTrap, LionPaws, and DoomTomb.

Clio picked up all three and brought them around to the picture side of the banner.

"Eight pictures, eight letters in each choice," Estella said, glaring at Dacey. "That has to mean something."

"Fine," said Dacey. "So it's not a rebus, but what's wrong with first impressions? It's not like we'll solve things bein' mute like him." Dacey pointed to Cameron.

"He gave us *da*," said Estella.

Cameron was in a no-win situation. If he stayed quiet, Dacey would be right. And if he spoke up now, she'd take the credit.

"Look," said Clio, pointing to the puzzle, saving him from Dacey. "Somehow, these objects spell out the answer, but I don't see it yet. 'Nest' starts with *N* and ends with *T*, and two of the choices have *N*'s, and two have *T*'s, but none of them start or end with those letters. In fact, none of the beginning letters of these pictures mesh with our choices. Anyone else?"

This would have been Cameron's opening, if he'd had something. Eight letters, eight objects. DoomTomb had repeated letters, but no objects repeated. Um, um . . . New tactic. If he were shooting these actual objects with his videocam, he'd focus on the straw of the nest next to soft bird feathers, then the rigid microscope with a human eye close to its lens. But that wasn't getting him anywhere.

"It's horrible," Dacey said. "My mind's stuck on that rebus idea, and it won't move off."

"Don't say that," said Estella, "or we'll all get stuck."

"I can talk," said Dacey. "I can talk about runnin' out of eggs and lookin' at plankton through a microscope, and what are all these nests in little rooms? Bird condo?"

"I think it's a chicken coop," said Cameron.

Dacey opened her eyes wide at him. "He speaks."

Cameron sucked in a breath.

"But not so much."

Estella gave her a dirty look. "He's right. Why else would there be a rooster?"

"Okay. So we can add chickens and eggs, and is anyone keepin' track of this?"

"No," said Clio, "but go on. You're doing good. It's making me think."

Dacey smiled. "So now there's an empty egg carton. It's like some of these have a theme and then not. You can't exactly connect nests and eggs with a sleeve or a teacup and saucer. But then we go back to the farm." She looked at Cameron. "What do you call that?"

"A hayloft?"

"Good call," said Dacey.

Cameron almost fainted from the shock of her compliment.

"And last, Mr. Interpreter of Pictures, you think that's a peapod?"

"Probably," said Cameron, "but it would help if they put some peas next to it."

"Well, duh," Dacey said. "Of course it would help."

Thank goodness he hadn't wasted a good faint on

her. He sneaked a look to see if anyone was snickering with her; but Clio was staring at the puzzle, and Estella was staring at Jig, who was sitting on the ground, leaning back on the fence with a smirk on his face.

"Lazy, good-for-nothing, like that pig I went out with," Estella said under her breath.

Either this wasn't Jig the Intense, or last year's TV people had created an illusion of intensity through the miracle of editing. They could have filmed Jig's fist-pumping when the Red Team guy twisted his ankle and Jig thought he might get in. Or when the goo hit Bianca and she had a brief meltdown. With the right footage, anyone could have made Jig look like a team player. Maybe he was the type who stayed lazy until he needed to get intense.

And now Dacey was on the ground, whispering to him. He could only hope she was trying to inspire him to bring his A game, but it looked like they were conspiring about something else. Forget them; otherwise, they'd all be doomed. DoomTomb doomed. Back to the puzzle.

Clio and Estella had been throwing around lame

ideas—about farms and things you find around the house—but at least they were talking. They weren't looking at this right, though. When he pretended with the videocam and added the bird and—

"It's like each picture is incomplete," he said under his breath, or so he thought.

Estella grabbed his arm. "Incomplete?"

"Yeah!" Clio said. "An egg carton without eggs and a nest without birds! Why'd they leave out the details?"

"There *is* a rooster in the chicken coop," said Estella.

Clio nodded. "But maybe he's there so we understand the picture. Like the pitchfork in the hayloft that doesn't have any hay. Maybe it's what's *missing* from the pictures." She patted him on the back.

Jig and Dacey came closer.

"Nice of you to join us," said Estella. "We are not your Little Red Hens."

"Huh?" said Jig.

"The story. No one would help the Little Red Hen bake her bread, so she ate it herself."

Dacey sighed. "Why on earth . . . ?"

"Look," Clio said. "This isn't divas on parade, and I'm talking to you, too, Jig. So either start working, or you two may as well let your alternates take your place."

"FYI," said Dacey, "we were working."

"On what?" said Estella.

Clio must have borrowed "the look" Cameron hated to see from his mom. But she used it for only a second. "So what's missing from each picture?"

Jig stepped up like he was suddenly running the show. "Picture number one, the bird's missing. Two, the microscope has a slide there, so maybe someone to look at it. Three, no chickens in the chicken house. Or hens, I should say. Little red hens, the three of you fine workers. Right, Estella?"

She ignored him.

"No eggs in the egg carton. Nothing to drink in the cup. A sleeve without the rest of the shirt or without an arm. No hay in the hayloft. And we can't see the peas in the pod."

"Who's we?" Estella said.

"Drop it." Clio went around the puzzle and came back with pens and paper. She handed them to

Cameron. "Write down what's missing as we repeat. Write it big."

He wrote as Clio dictated.

1. *Bird*
2. *Person*
3. *Chicken/hen*
4. *Eggs*
5. *Drink*
6. *Arm/shirt*
7. *Hay*
8. *Peas*

"It still doesn't spell anything," said Dacey.

Even Estella didn't give her the stink eye.

"I don't want to be rude and think out loud again." Dacey paused and looked at Estella.

"Go ahead."

"But it's hard for me to shut my mouth and be productive at the same time. It seems the list is both specific and general."

"What does that mean?" asked Estella.

Dacey shot her a glance.

"No, really, genuinely," Estella said. "Explain."

"Chickens, eggs, arms, hay, and peas are objects. Birds and people and drinks are categories. So maybe we need to get specific with those, too."

"Let's say you're right," said Jig, "but how will that spell JinxTrap or LionPaws or DoomTomb?"

"Remember," said Clio, "eight pictures and eight letters. How do we turn each picture into a letter?" She looked at Dacey. "Let's keep going with your specifics. So, birds."

"We should skip that one for now," said Estella, "or we'll be here all day naming species. For the microscope. Scientist? Researcher?"

"Or really specific," said Clio, "an eye. And from the teacup, there's no tea. Tea. Eye."

That was it! "Jay," said Cameron.

"Like a blue jay!" Clio shouted.

"What?" said Estella.

"The missing object is spelling out the choice," Clio said. "Jay like a blue jay in the nest. An eye for the microscope."

"What's with the chicken then?" Dacey asked.

"It's a hen. An *N*," said Jig. "And 'eggs' sounds

like *X*. JinxTrap!" He grabbed it.

Estella clamped her hand on his wrist. "Wait. Take two seconds. Spell the rest out."

"*T* in the cup. 'Arm' sounds like *R*. 'Hay,' like *A*. And a pea is a *P*."

Estella let go. "Open it!"

Stunt #2
✱ ✱ ✱ ✱ ✱ ✱ ✱ ✱ ✱ ✱ ✱

First, it was pigs; now it's the mice.

We promise, you'll only see animals twice.

The rodents have rabidly jumped

from their cages

And need to be stopped or

they'll throw violent rages.

Don't touch them, we warn you;

their bites all can kill.

Use the sticks or the tongs or

the fork or the drill.

You can use any tool that you find

on the ground,

then keep trapping mice until

each one is found.

"I saw the trap," said Dacey. "It's somewhere near a pencil."

"This way!" said Clio. She led them past the giant school supplies. How could she remember without a map?

"Hey, Dacey," said Jig, "if you knew JinxTrap was here, why didn't you say so?"

"Because it's also near a tomb and a lion. Just because I'm blond doesn't mean I'm stupid." She turned left. A domed cage towered in front of them. Its wide-set bars curved about ten feet upward to a point on the top, and it had fifteen oval indents in its brass base.

"That's three mice apiece," said Jig. "Where are they?"

"And where are the tools we need?" Dacey asked.

Close to the cage were a collection of tombstones, a basket of oversized food, four bedroom dressers stacked on top of one another, a lion lying on a small cave, and a crazy amount of other objects.

It was like one of those picture search-and-finds. Where's the necktie in the jungle scene? Or the mop on the ocean floor? And here, in real time, where were the mice in the warehouse? It could make a person dizzy.

Cameron opened one of the dresser drawers. Nothing. Another. Yeah! There was a mouse the size of a giant wedge of Swiss cheese. "Found one!" he called.

The others raced over.

"So that's what they look like," said Clio.

"What are you waiting for?" said Estella. "Get it in the cage."

There had to be some tool near here, something he could use to pick up the furry gray thing. He opened another drawer. No mouse, no tool. Another drawer. A hammer! He reached in, then shut the drawer fast.

The instructions said they could use any tool they found on the *floor*. But where on the floor? Maybe over in the—

Bzzzz!

The mouse in Cameron's drawer lit up red with the words, *You touched me. 5-minute penalty. Ha-ha-ha!*

"Look what she did!" said Dacey. "How lazy can you be, Estella! You cost us!"

"I forgot. I'm sorry," said Estella. "You turned

away, Cameron. I thought you were too squeamish to touch the thing. I just wanted to help. To hurry. I'm sorry."

Clio rushed over and gave her a quick hug. "It's okay."

"This is not the love and comfort show," Jig said. "Just go! Everyone. Find mice! Find tools! And touch only the tools on the floor or I'll kill you."

Cameron raced to the cave. Inside were a mouse and one of those big barbecue forks. It would be too homicidal maniac to stab the mouse, so he used the fork to push it against the cave wall; then he slid the tines underneath and lifted it inch by inch. The mouse wasn't all that light, and it didn't come close to fitting on the fork, but Cameron had it well balanced. He took three small steps, and the mouse fell off.

"Hey, buddy," said Jig, running by with a mouse between a pair of tongs, "the rules don't say anything about carrying it."

"Right." Cameron leaned over and used the fork as a hockey stick, letting the mouse slide as far as each shot would take it, being careful not to slap it into someone's foot. He didn't need another five-minute major penalty.

It took nine swipes to get the mouse to the cage, then a solid prodding to get it onto the inch-high base and into one of the indents. Jig's and another were already in place.

It was good to spread out, not be in one another's faces. But now where? Had anyone taken the lit-up mouse from the drawer? No.

Cameron flipped the mouse out and pretended he was gliding down the ice for the game-winning goal. "He shoots, he scores!"

Six mice in. Back to the dressers.

Each one had two drawers on the bottom, three in the middle, and three shallower ones on top. He checked the other drawers in the lowest dresser and the bottom two rows in the second one. Nothing but another decoy tool. He wasn't tall enough to see inside the higher drawers, and he didn't want to reach in, feel around, and accidentally touch a mouse.

He opened the lowest drawers and used them as steps. Nothing in the next tier. He tried climbing higher, but it felt unstable.

Cameron cleared his throat. "Anyone see a ladder?" he called.

No answer. He'd find something himself.

Jig whipped around with another mouse between his tongs. "I found this one in the lion's mouth," he said. "No ladder, but Humpty Dumpty's behind the cave. You can probably stand on his wall." Jig raced toward the cage. Cameron went the other way.

Nothing in the rules about knocking Humpty off, but what if they needed him later? Cameron placed the egg on the ground and tested the stone wall to see if it would move. The stones were plastic or something. He pushed the wall to the dresser and hoisted himself up. No mice in the third dresser. None in the bottom two rows on the fourth. In the last drawer, yes!

Cameron flicked that mouse out with his fork.

Again he played mouse hockey and sent it over the cage bottom with a mighty slap shot. A little finesse put the rodent in its groove. He turned to see Estella stretched under some bushes near the tombs. "Are you okay?"

She lifted her head. "There's one here. Can't quite reach it. Trade my chopsticks for your fork?"

They made the swap just before Dacey and Clio came with a mouse each. That would be twelve and thirteen. Estella's would be—

"Can you believe this?" Dacey pointed to Estella.

Estella was now on her stomach, her head resting on one arm, the fork an inch from the mouse.

"Jig!" Dacey called.

He came around. "You found it."

"No," Dacey said. "I found this." She pointed again. "First, she's so lazy, picking up the mouse with her hands, and now, napping at a time like this."

"No," Cameron said. "She's getting a mouse."

His words, though, were drowned out by Dacey, who hadn't stopped talking. "Fine, Serio. You take your little siesta. Leave us to do the work. I swear, all of you are so lazy."

Estella scooted out from the bushes and bolted up. Her face was redder than anyone's Cameron had seen before. She balled up her fist. "All of you, who?"

"Catfight!" Jig called.

Clio jumped between the two and grabbed Estella's hand. She kept it in her grip as she turned to Dacey. "Tell me I didn't hear you right. Tell me you weren't labeling her or her family. Tell me you're not that ugly."

Dacey's nose twitched. "Seriously? You think that's what I meant?" she said sweet as syrup. "I didn't mean anything by it. I swear. If delicate people like Estella need to take a rest instead of faintin'—"

"You think we're that stupid?" said Clio. "Maybe we should ask Bill to roll back the footage to see if I need hearing aids or you need major attitude training." She took a step back. "This is how it's going to work. This team is going to win. And that's going to happen because you, Dacey, are going to cut the comments and the bickering and focus on what we need to do."

Dacey held back most of a gasp.

"Estella, take a breath. Get that mouse. It's almost out of the bushes."

Estella closed her eyes, took a very deep breath, and dropped back to the ground.

"And Jig, I heard you telling Dacey your little plan to slack off early so you can swoop in and be a big hero in the end. Forget it. Go find that last mouse. P.S. You may want to work on your whispering skills." Clio ran off.

Jig smiled and shrugged.

Cameron almost wished Spencer were here instead of Jig. He couldn't make that happen, but he could find the last mouse. The others had spread away from the cage. He stayed close and circled, focusing on the ground. Circled again with focus at knee level. Focus, shoulder level. Focus, higher. There!

"Jig!" he called, his voice feeling more powerful since Clio had spoken up. "Need your height. The last mouse is on top of the cage."

Footsteps. But it was Clio, then Dacey, then Estella with a skewered mouse on the fork. "Still have the chopsticks, Cameron?"

He held them out to her just as Jig ran up.

Jig pointed to Estella. "Mouse kebab! And this from someone who didn't want to kick a fake pig."

"I was picturing something other than a helpless animal."

Dacey gave her the fakest smile Cameron had ever seen.

"Ha!" Jig stepped onto a giant strawberry Clio had thought to drag underneath the last mouse and reached a screwdriver through the bars of the cage. "Not long enough. I'll need that fork, Estella."

Estella used the chopsticks to pry the mouse off the fork and handed it to Jig. "Clear out," he said. "I'm going to shove it. If it touches you, it's your fault."

Within five seconds he'd poked that mouse off the top and it had fallen through the cage's bars. Estella ran in with the chopsticks and moved it to the last groove.

Lights flashed. "Exit the trap," said a woman's voice. "Exit the trap. Clear the area."

They stepped back. Clamps rose from the ground and bolted down the mice. The cage's bars lifted.

Where was the puzzle, though? Not up from the floor. Not down from the ceiling.

Then Cameron saw it, something white curled inside one of the holes where bars used to be. "Please be Puzzle Number Three," he whispered.

Cameron dug the curled envelope from the hole while the others were still sort of spinning in circles.

"Got it," he said.

They gathered around.

Puzzle #3

* * * * * * * * * * *

I Sue Pret hurt some needy weak puzzle doers

(Your choices are behind the cave.)

"Where behind the cave?" said Jig. "I was all over it."

Behind them, clear as day, was a blue-lit table

with their choices: RetroWars, Super Sneeze, and Supreme Dazzlers.

"This table was not here before. I swear."

"It wasn't," said Clio.

"Bill?" Jig called to the air. "You carry this thing in?"

Cameron knelt on the floor and ran his finger around the corner of a hairline seam. "The floor opens," he said. "Like how they bring things up onstage."

"He's right." Bill came from behind a creepy clown face. "But don't spoil our secrets, okay? Anyway, bad penalty, huh, Estella?"

She hung her head.

"You'd be better off without it, but the mouse on the cage landed on an Orange kid's head. So you're even there. The problem is, the Orange Team isn't talking smack, which, most likely, is why you're six minutes behind. Play smart, play nice, okay?" He turned and disappeared into the clown's mouth.

"He's right," said Estella. "My fault. Some of it. I'm done with that." She pointed. "The puzzle. What do you think?"

"I think it's a confession." Jig cleared his throat. "I, Sue Pret, do guiltily admit that I hurt some nerds." He laughed at his own lameness.

"C'mon, Jig," said Estella. "You heard Bill. You trying to lose this thing?"

"He's not," Dacey said too fast. "Your sense of humor take that vacation? Or did your brains?"

"Oh, no," said Clio. "Just stop." She pointed to the words *I Sue Pret hurt some needy weak puzzle doers*—it didn't even look like a sentence.

"Besides the fact it's missing a bunch of punctuation—"

"Like Lavinia noticed last year," said Dacey. "She was such a geek, but so smart. Did you see her at regionals? She's prettier than I thought she could ever be."

"And the reason that's important?" said Estella.

Clio shot her a look.

"Sorry," Estella said. "*Now* I'm done. Punctuation? I say no. They wouldn't give us a rerun from last year."

"Agreed," said Jig. "But it's still weird. What kind of name is Sue Pret? They didn't pick it out of nowhere."

Obviously. Or maybe it was obvious only to Cameron. "They made up that name so they could spell the choices."

Clio leaned into the puzzle. "He's right! You're right!" She pointed and spelled at the same time: "R-E-T-R-O-W-A-R-S." All the letters were in the sentence, in order. "Wait. Supreme Dazzlers and Super Sneeze are in order, too!"

"Which is a major big problem," said Dacey, "because we're no closer than we were ten years ago."

"Sure we are," said Clio. "It gives us a place to start."

Dacey shook her head. "What if it's coincidence?"

"They don't give us puzzle instructions," said Jig, "so they have to give us something."

They stood around the puzzle. Not even Dacey was thinking out loud.

The silence, though, let Cameron think. All the letters of each choice were in order, but not in any noticeable pattern. Not every other letter or every third letter or anything like that and—

"All I know," Dacey said, breaking the silence, "if it's Supreme Dazzlers, I'll rock the stunt. Every year when the new version came out, I'd beg my mama to buy it. And she did. But my luck it'll be Super Sneeze and we'll have to crawl into some snot-filled nose."

Jig laughed. "The nose is over in that far corner. I saw it."

"Gross."

"But none of that brings us closer to the answer," said Estella.

"Right," Clio said. "So all the letters of all three choices . . ."

Cameron started to raise his hand, but that was stupid. "Um." He scratched his head instead. "I was trying to see if every third letter or sixth letter or something like that spelled out one of the choices, but I don't see a pattern yet."

Jig tapped his finger on the puzzle paper. "Okay, okay."

Cameron looked again.

I Sue Pret hurt some needy weak puzzle doers

"Thank goodness we're not looking for hidden meanings in the words," said Dacey.

Cameron tried to ignore her or anything that didn't push them forward.

"There are thirty-six letters in this wonky sentence," Jig said, running with Cameron's thought. "If we number the letters, in order from one to thirty-six, maybe we'll find something."

"I have good penmanship," said Dacey. "I'll write it down." She spaced the letters across two rows. Below them, she wrote the corresponding numbers.

```
I S u e P r e t h u r t s o m e n e e d y
1 2 3 4 5 6 7 8 9 10 11 12 13 14 15 16 17 18 19 20 21

w e a k p u z z l e d o e r s
22 23 24 25 26 27 28 29 30 31 32 33 34 35 36
```

Meanwhile, Cameron wrote the numbers that corresponded to the letters in RetroWars: 6, 7, 8, 11, 14, 24, 35, 36.

Clio stood right next to him. "What's this, Cameron?"

"RetroWars with its corresponding number form, but I don't see a pattern."

"Explain," said Estella. "Why did you use seven for the *E*? The four is an *E*, and so are the sixteen and all those others."

"The choices are all spelled out in order," said Cameron. "So the *E* we use has to come after the first *R* and before the first *T*. Otherwise, we'd be jumping all over the place."

"Right," said Clio. "Okay, everyone. So Cameron wrote the numbers that correspond to RetroWars. Look for some pattern while we write the numbers of the other two."

Cameron took on Supreme Dazzlers: 2, 3, 5, 6, 7, 15, 16 (or 18 or 19), 24, 28, 29, 31 (or 34), 35, 36.

"I don't see anything here," he said, "but it's confusing. Two of the letters can have different numbers."

"And Super Sneeze has options for the last four." Clio slid her paper to him: 2, 3, 5, 7, 11, 13, 17, 18/19, 19/23, 28/29, 31/34

"RetroWars is the only one with exact letter-number matches, right?" said Estella. "You think that's anything?

Silence.

"Yeah," said Estella. "I didn't think so, either."

"Anyone want to trade number sequences?" Jig asked. "I got nothing here."

Cameron didn't want to. There was something about this one, about Super Sneeze. It started with seven no-choice numbers: 2, 3, 5, 7, 11, 13, 17. All odd except for the 2. Then came four numbers with choices, but one option was always odd. If only he could get rid of that stinkin' 2. He slammed the paper to the table.

"What?" said Clio.

"Super Sneeze? All the numbers could be odd except they had to throw in that two to spoil everything."

Clio turned the paper toward her. "You're good," she said. "He's good," she said louder so everyone could hear.

"He got it?" Dacey asked.

"He got me to get it. Look," said Clio.

And Cameron saw it, too. "Prime numbers," he said. "Super Sneeze can be made with all the prime numbers in the sentence."

"That's a math thing, right?" said Dacey.

"Yeah," said Estella. "Prime numbers: any numbers higher than one, divisible only by one and its own self."

Cameron waited for some rude comment, but nothing came.

"But what about the option numbers in Super Sneeze?" Dacey said. "Y'all think we can ignore those?"

"I say we go with it. Make up some time. Hey, you Golly people!" Jig looked toward the ceiling as if they'd be there. "We logically think the letters in Super Sneeze correspond to prime numbers. If we're wrong, don't give us a penalty. Okay?"

Silence.

"You expected an answer?" Dacey said.

"Why are you trying so hard to get on everyone's nerves?" Jig opened Super Sneeze.

Stunt #3
* * * * * * * * * * *

Primed for passing?

Yes? No?

The nose knows.

"It's the giant nose," Jig said in Dacey's face. Then he took off toward the far corner.

There it was. A nose taller than Cameron, its nostrils like twin tunnels. To the side was another card over a playpen of footballs.

Stunt #3
* * * * * * * * * * *

It's really quite simple a stunt.
You don't need to run or to punt.
Just pass ten of those
through our very big nose,
then stand three feet out from its front.

***Additional rules: (1) Each person must pass one ball into each nostril from behind the blue line; to count, the ball must remain fully inside the nostril. (2) When you've accomplished that, stand three feet from the nose in the marked green area. (3) You should soon know what to do next.

Jig already had a ball in each hand. "Let's throw snot balls into the nose. Blue line's way back here."

It was at least twenty feet away. Cameron grabbed two balls, and so did the others.

"Holy gracious me!" said Dacey. "I need to throw a football all the way there? I can do lots of things, but holy gracious me."

"It's better than searching inside a snot-filled nose," said Estella.

Dacey laughed. "Sure as spit."

"We'll figure out a way to help you," said Clio.

Jig got behind the line. The others watched. "I'm not the sideshow," he said. "Someone throw to the other nostril." And he launched a perfect spiral into his.

Clio heaved back and got hers in, too. "It's a huge target. Just go for it."

Jig made his second, and Cameron stepped up from behind him. He took a big heave and launched the football too high in the air.

"Not so much adrenaline," said Jig, running to fetch the ball.

Clio got her second one in, and Estella stepped up next. "Don't watch," she said. "I throw like a girl."

"You are a girl," said Dacey.

"Still doesn't mean I want to throw like one."

Cameron put his second ball down so he could get a better feel for this. He took a look at his target and

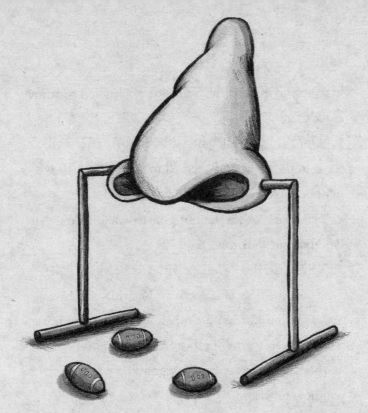

visualized the way Spencer might throw the ball. His
pass came off a little wobbly, but it hit the mark.

Estella's fell short.

"Throw your second one, Estella," Clio said.
"We'll get you another."

Jig was already chasing after it.

Estella threw, this time underhanded. The ball
arced up and up and came down just in time to clear
the opening.

Cameron stepped from behind her and got

his second in. He moved aside to make room for Dacey.

"Don't laugh, y'all," she said. She twisted her whole torso to the right and seemed to throw the ball with her body. No extension of her arm.

"So I guess they taught you to wave in pageant land but not to throw," said Jig.

"Oh, I can throw kisses with the best of them."

"Show me how you do that," he said.

Dacey put her hand on her hip. "I get the point. You can stop teasin' me."

"No teasing," said Jig. "I'm gonna use that to teach you how to throw."

"Fine." Dacey put her hand to her mouth, then flung it toward the heavens.

"Good. Good," said Jig. "Same motion, but just the reverse. Hold the ball to the outside of your body, then do the kissing motion forward."

Dacey tried, but the ball sailed way to the left.

Jig stood next to her. "You have distance, and I have a new tactic. Use your normal kiss-throwing motion, but"—he grabbed her shoulders and turned her so her right side faced the nostril—"start with the ball at your waist, as if your lips were there; then throw that kiss."

The ball bounced short, then sideways, then back, then it rolled and rolled and *in!*

"Do it again," he said.

It took her three more tries, but she got it.

"You done, Estella?" said Jig.

"I took care of it while you were all watching the Dacey show."

"Everyone!" Clio called. "Green area!"

They squeezed in. Steam poured from the nose. It let out some gasps. *"Ah-ah-ah."* It stopped. *"Ah-choo!"* Out flew hundreds of slime-covered, acorn-sized brown balls, dodgeball style.

Dacey started retreating, but Cameron grabbed her arm and held her in the green area.

The slime balls stopped coming. Now what? Nothing came. No clue, no lights, no noises, no nothing.

"Bless you?" Clio said to the nose.

Out shot some boxes of tissues.

"Don't tell me we need to wipe the slime balls," Estella said. "I wipe enough boogery noses at home." She pulled out a hunk of tissues and wiped one ball down anyway.

Cameron followed her lead. So gross, but underneath the slime? Words.

CHAPTER 22

If they needed every slime ball for the next puzzle, they'd be hunting them down through Thanksgiving. All the balls they saw, though, had the same two words: "green wall."

Three of the warehouse walls were sky blue; only the fourth was the color of grass. Without saying a word, they raced toward the front corner, then made their way along the green wall. A table near the middle had their choices: Who's There?, Things that Go Bump, and Baby Chat-a-Lot.

Bill jumped off a refrigerator.

Dacey screamed.

"Good," said Bill. "You're awake."

"Great job on the nose, but not good enough. You picked up only thirty-one seconds. Somehow, you need to find nearly five and a half minutes or I'll be wearing my little maid outfit for a year. And that could be ugly. Now go!"

Estella opened the envelope.

Puzzle #4
✱ ✱ ✱ ✱ ✱ ✱ ✱ ✱ ✱ ✱ ✱

trenchcoat bookmark window whiplash however bubbly igloo otter noodles scratchy nefarious xylophone serpent elephant trunk tickle trench hurricane eyewash frumpy artichoke femur ragamuffin hopscotch butterscotch moss projectile meanwhile end

"Well, this is pretty much garbage," she said. "It's like they threw the dictionary into a shredder."

"Only after they let a bunch of words escape," said Clio. "Why these?"

"Isn't that the point of the puzzle?" Dacey said.

Clio took in a deep breath. "Right," she said on exhale.

"At least *end* is at the end," Jig said.

"Which isn't good," said Estella. "If it weren't at the end, it might give us the tape bump."

"The what?" Dacey had that tone in her voice again.

Cameron tensed, but Clio leaned in, ready to handle it.

"You have a roll of tape, but you can't find the end, right? Then you hold it to the light and see where to pick at it to get it going. That's the tape bump."

Cameron liked the comparison, but Dacey's mouth was gearing up to disagree. Five minutes. They needed to make up five minutes. He needed to head her off. "You mean, a clue," he said. "Like how the first two words are compound words. So are some of the others." He'd already thrown away that idea, but anything to stop the sniping.

Estella nodded.

"So, compound words," said Dacey. "That's our tape bump?"

If he said no, she'd probably yell at him for throwing out a lame idea. "Um, well . . ."

"So that's a no," she said.

"Pretty much."

"Then why—"

Clio took a step toward her. "It's called brainstorming, Dacey. And now we know: no compound words. No definitions, either. Too many words to connect. They wouldn't do that."

"They can be mean," said Dacey.

"Not that mean."

Not counting the ongoing crackle of tension, it was quiet. Even so, Cameron wanted to find that cave and buy himself some space to find the tape bump.

"Some of the words look connected," Estella said, apparently ignoring the tension. *Window* and *whiplash* both start with *W.*"

"And?"

"I wasn't finished, Dacey, because there's *elephant trunk*, which is a term. And *hurricane eyewash*. And before you say anything, I know hurricanes don't wash their eyes. All I'm saying, there's such a thing as a hurricane eye, and it's interesting how those words are in that order. Also *hopscotch* and *butterscotch*, both end the same. And *projectile* and *meanwhile*."

"But what does that mean?" Dacey asked.

"I'm just throwing it out there. Isn't that what we do?"

"Fine."

There was something in what Estella just said. Cameron wiggled his fingers in the air as if he could almost feel a bump.

"Twenty-nine words," said Jig.

"Huh?" Estella said.

"There're twenty-nine words in this puzzle. None of the choices have that many letters, but like the last puzzle, all the letters of all our choices appear in order."

"They wouldn't do that again," Clio said. "That's not how they work."

"Unless it is," said Dacey. "What if they're trying to throw us off?"

Clio gave a small nod. "Possible."

It was possible. At least it was a place to start. First on the table: Who's There? All the letters in order. There were two *W*'s in *window*, then a third, immediately, in *whiplash*, which had two *H*'s. And the second *H* butted up to the *H* in *however*. He put his index finger near the adjoining *W*'s and his middle finger on the neighboring *H*'s. *O*'s next. It was swimming with them: *bookmark*, then *igloo otter noodles*. Two together, three in a row, then two more. But the choices had only one *O* each.

"Hmm," he said, or breathed, really. "Could be two letters together, just not—"

"Don't get all quiet on me," said Clio. "What are you thinking?"

He turned to her. "It's—"

"No," she said. "Faster if you say it to everyone."

They were all looking at him.

"I'm not sure if I'll make sense and—"

"Just spit it out," said Dacey.

"Double letters. There are all these double letters."

He pulled the puzzle toward him.

trenchcoat bookmark window whiplash however bubbly igloo otter noodles scratchy nefarious xylophone serpent elephant trunk tickle trench hurricane eyewash frumpy artichoke femur ragamuffin hopscotch butterscotch moss projectile meanwhile end

"It's almost like double letters in this list spell out a choice, but there are too many double *O*'s. Even a triple *O*."

Silence. They kept looking at him.

"Explain," Jig said.

"I keep wanting to use double letters to spell the name of, say, Who's There?" said Cameron. "First letter, *W*. *Window* ends in a *W*, and *whiplash* starts with a *W*. So two *W*'s together. But that means we've already thrown away the first set of double letters, the *O*'s in *bookmark*, and none of our choices start with *O*."

A pair of arms had him in a headlock. But it wasn't Spencer. It was Jig. "You got it."

"But—"

"Forget all the double letters. It's when one letter

ends a word and the same letter starts the next one. *Those* letters spell out *this!*" Jig bonked Cameron's head with Who's There?, then opened the box.

None of the game's pieces were inside; just small, black boxes, each with a single button in its center. Remotes. At least that's what they looked like. Also a small card:

Stunt #4
* * * * * * * * * * *

Point your signalers to the top of the green wall. Press your buttons at the exact same time (or as exact as humanly possible). You'll know if you weren't exact enough. No penalty for trying again, unless you count the time you wasted. Go!

Jig handed out the signalers. "On three. One, two, three!"

They pressed, but nothing happened.

"Again," said Jig. "One, two, three!"

Nothing.

"Who's not pressing at the same time?" he said.

"Here!" said Clio.

"Then get it right," Dacey said.

"No. Here on the back. There's an arrow! Find your arrow, and point it toward the ceiling. One, two, three!"

The green wall started parting in the middle, slowly, spotlights swirling overhead, revealing behind it a glimpse of yellow and orange and—

"It's the Rainbow Maze!" said Jig. "They let me try it last year. It's incredible, it's fierce, it's—"

Estella gasped. "It's the pig."

Behind the wall stood a guy.

Estella turned to Clio. "What's he doing here? Stephen. My ex-boyfriend." She reached over and dug her nails into Cameron's arm. "Oh my gosh! He's my person. When they interviewed us, who we didn't want to compete against . . ." She shook her head and let go. "Why didn't I put my best friend?"

Lined up behind him were two girls and then . . .

Cameron felt a little ill. "It's my brother Spencer. He does not lose."

Before the wall finished opening, a voice came from nowhere. "You have three free minutes to greet your visitors. Your game clock will pause, starting . . . now!"

Spencer ran up and thumped him on the back. "Your team's losing, dude."

"Why do you have to rub it in?"

"Because I'm so good at it." Spencer grinned. "So what are you gonna do about it?"

"I don't know. It's hard with . . ." Cameron looked in Dacey's direction.

She was all smiles around her person, her very beautiful, very tall person.

"Dude. Just deal with Dacey," said Spencer. "Clio is."

Clio was jumping around with her friend, and she'd included Estella with them. The ex-boyfriend was standing by himself, tapping the shell of the four-foot ladybug.

"So, when did you find out about this?" Cameron asked Spencer.

"They told me and Clio's friend this morning after you left us. The other three jokers found out yesterday and had private planes pick them up. Lucky." Spencer shook his head. "Hey, what do you think about him?"

"Who?

Spencer turned Cameron's head toward Jig and his person.

"I've seen that smirk somewhere before," Cameron said. "Holy cow!"

Spencer laughed. "Can you believe Golly had the guts to bring back the cheater?"

Jig and Rocky Titus were heading straight toward them, laughing over something.

It got Dacey's attention, too. She looked straight at Jig. "Why him?"

"Because I'm me," said Rocky.

"Meet Rocky. Toughest competitor I've ever seen, and I've seen a lot."

"Not tougher than mine." Dacey switched on a smile and reached out to the tall girl. "Meet Laura Ramirez, ultimate pageant queen and my competition again, it appears."

"I'm Spencer. Cameron's my brother."

"And this," Clio said, "is my best friend, Janae. Whatever I don't know, she does. Whatever I can't do, she can."

Estella shook her head. "That, over there, is Stephen and—"

"You have twenty seconds," the voice said.

"And," said Clio to Estella, "you were saved by the voice."

Their little circle started breaking up, the Blue Team backing a bit toward one side, the new people toward the other.

"Three, two, one, and start!"

The giant ladybug buzzed, sending Stephen stumbling way back. One of the ladybug's legs came forward with a big envelope: "STUNT #4."

Clio took the envelope, slid her finger under the flap, and winced. Blood was already rising from the paper cut, but she pulled out the card and read out loud:

Who's There?
Now you see who's here!
It's a face-off between each pair.
One-on-one combat.
Your challenge will begin in 3 MINUTES.
WHERE: You'll find ten computer monitors farther down the wall.
HOW TO PLAY: Your monitors will show a sea

of faces. Study them. After 30 seconds they will disappear; then, one at a time, 5 faces will appear. For each face, answer yes or no: Did you see that person in the group picture?

WHY YOU WANT TO WIN: Every Blue Team member who wins his or her one-on-one will earn your team an easier versus harder piece to the next puzzle.

WHY THEY WILL TRY TO BEAT YOU: They will receive money. Thousands of dollars. And if they try to let you win? No money for them, and 25 penalty minutes for you. How will we know if they're slacking? We know how fast they should go. We gave them two warm-up rounds and recorded their speed. Now walk to your monitors.

That was all Cameron needed: a warmed-up Spencer. "Warm-up round?"

"They had us do the same thing with a group of animals, then junk in a desk. They told us to go our fastest, but I didn't know it counted for anything."

"You'd never take it easy on me anyway."

"I might have. The more you win, the more you'll give me."

Cameron shook his head.

A woman's voice came out of nowhere. "You have two minutes. Please find the monitor with your name. Blue Team will be on the blue side of the table; guests, on the white side."

The setup had them face-to-face with their direct competitors, the monitors their only buffers.

Estella was glaring at her ex-boyfriend.

Clio and Janae were chatting about a trip to Washington, D.C.

Rocky and Jig were laughing at each other.

Dacey's plastered-on smile looked like it might crack her face.

"You know you're going down," said Spencer across the two monitors.

Cameron took a deep breath and managed to look him directly in the eye. "Not if I can help it."

Cameron's screen started a countdown. "3. 2. 1. Go!"

His monitor showed twenty kids on four rows of risers. Boys, girls. Every hair color; every skin shade;

every type of clothing. He stared and stared, but how could he remember all twenty? What would happen if he didn't? Spencer would have bragging rights again, that's what. Nine seconds left. Tan girl, medium blond hair. Asian boy with black glasses. Kid who grinned like Walker. Girl with a mole near her lip. Dark-skinned girl with bright green—

The screen went blank to a chorus of groans.

"Finally!" said Spencer.

Cameron suspected that was for effect, but he couldn't let Spencer's confidence, fake or not, suck all his concentration.

The screen lit back up with the kid who grinned like Walker. Underneath him it read: "Was this person in the picture? Yes/No."

Cameron touched Yes.

Next, a girl with medium brown hair and a pink shirt. He didn't remember her, but he couldn't rule her out. What should he do? Really, time was what mattered. He touched No. The computer didn't buzz him wrong. Was that a good sign?

Next. A boy in a baseball cap with a purple *M*. He remembered the cap, but was it *that* boy? Just go. Yes.

Tan girl, medium blond hair. Yes.

Asian girl, black glasses. Yes? No. The black glasses were on the Asian boy.

The screen blanked, then blinked back on. "4/5. Almost. Try, try again."

"Doing great over here, Cameron," Spencer said. "Doing good?"

Cameron didn't answer. He touched the screen, and all the people came back. Twenty seconds on the clock. And that girl with the pink shirt *was* there. Would they give them the same five kids? Probably not. He studied harder. The boy with the white shirt who looked like a thousand people. The kid who was a little cross-eyed. One who looked like his friend Franklin. One who looked like Darla from algebra, one—

Blank screen. Same choices?

Nope.

"Oh, man," he heard Estella's boyfriend say. "Different people."

"I got it this time," said Spencer. "Beat me, Cameron. Just try."

Cameron wished he had earplugs. Okay. Pale boy with freckles. Never saw him.

Girl with a pink streak in her hair. No.

Girl with the mole. Yes!

Bright green shirt. Yes!

Dark-skinned boy who looked like his friend Sameer. No!

That had to be right. The monitor went blank. It blinked back on: "5/5 but sorry. Spencer beat you by 0.3 second. Please take a seat in the blue chairs and remain silent."

It was just Spencer and him making their way to ten blue chairs. If he'd been up against anyone else, he would have won.

Sorry, Spencer mouthed. But that smile wasn't the least bit sorry.

Cameron had just sat when Clio trotted over, arms raised in victory. Janae came around, and they gave each other a big hug.

Clio raised her eyebrows. *You win?* she mouthed.

Cameron shook his head.

She patted him on the back anyway.

In just moments it was apparent that Dacey had lost to Laura, that Jig had won and Estella had, too. She took a chair as far away as possible from Stephen.

Now what? How long were they supposed to be silent?

"*A-a-ahh!*" Bill ran out from near the Rainbow Maze, arms and legs flailing like a crazy man.

They all laughed.

"It was so quiet here," he said. "I couldn't stand it. Say good-bye to our visitors. You'll see them again in a little while." He handed Estella an envelope. "If you want to, that is."

"Come, visitors!" He walked them back toward the Rainbow Maze wall.

Before Estella could open the envelope, Bill turned around. "You picked up a minute thirty-nine. Now go!"

CHAPTER 23

"W'e're less than four behind," said Jig. "We can do this."

"We can," Clio said.

"We can," Cameron echoed with the other two.

Estella held out the puzzle card.

Puzzle #5
* * * * * * * * * * *

Your questions and choices are near
the huge blue entry door.

They took off, but when they rounded the sailboat, there was no blue-lit table. There were three blue-lit doors. Embedded in each was a framed screen lit with a string of five numbers, all ones and twos.

Dacey reached for a doorknob.

Clio flew in front of her. "No. What if opening one is like opening a box?"

Dacey backed away. "You're right."

Jig had peeled their envelope off a suit of armor. He read its card aloud.

Puzzle #5

＊ ＊ ＊ ＊ ＊ ＊ ＊ ＊ ＊ ＊

Congratulations! You have earned three easier questions for this round! Answer all five questions correctly and you will know which door to open. Open only that door.

P.S. Need a hint?

And there was a small right-pointing arrow at the bottom of the card. Jig turned it over. "There's nothing here."

"They tease," said Dacey. "But where are the questions?"

One arm from the suit of armor rose and pointed

behind them to a bank of five more monitors mounted on a wall. Each read "Touch Here."

Clio touched the one on the left, and the screen fully lit.

QUESTION #1

HOW MANY COUNTRIES COUNT GLACIERS AS PART OF THEIR TERRITORY?

CHOOSE 1 IF THAT ANSWER IS GREATER THAN 18.

CHOOSE 2 IF THAT ANSWER IS EQUAL TO OR LESS THAN 18.

"I still don't see a hint," said Dacey. "Where's . . . our . . . hint?" she called to the ceiling.

"Did you expect an answer?" asked Estella.

"C'mon," said Clio. "Maybe we don't need a hint. Glaciers. All I know is they're massive bodies of ice and provide water and are shrinking with global warming."

"If only my brother George were here," said Estella. "He's got this thing about icebergs and glaciers. Rain forests, too."

"What if we start naming countries with glaciers," Clio said. "Up in Alaska, so the United States. Canada. Antarctica. Greenland."

"Iceland?" said Dacey.

"Don't know," Clio said. "We learned Iceland is green and Greenland is icy. Anyone?"

"Russia," said Cameron. "China, I think."

Dacey sighed. "If that's an easy question, we are in serious trouble."

"Maybe not," said Clio. "The doors will tell us."

"Because doors talk," said Dacey.

"No. Suppose the answer to question five is definitely two. If only one door has a two in the fifth position, it's the right door. I say we go to the next question." Clio touched the second screen.

QUESTION #2

WHAT IS A NORMAL DECIBEL LEVEL FOR EVERY-DAY CONVERSATION?

CHOOSE 1 IF THAT ANSWER IS GREATER THAN 85.

CHOOSE 2 IF THAT ANSWER IS EQUAL TO OR
LESS THAN 85.

"Over eighty-five in my house," said Jig, "over eighty-five hundred probably."

That wasn't right. Cameron started raising his hand again, but his mouth took over. "I was at a basketball game with a decibel meter. It only got as high as one-fifteen, and it was deafening in there. It's probably number two."

"Are you absolutely positive?" said Jig.

"Ninety percent," Cameron said.

"Right now we need one hundred," said Jig.

They moved to the next monitor.

QUESTION #3

HOW MANY DIMPLES IN A STANDARD GOLF
BALL?

CHOOSE 1 IF THAT ANSWER IS GREATER THAN
200.

CHOOSE 2 IF THAT ANSWER IS EQUAL TO OR
LESS THAN 200.

* * * *

"Seriously?" Dacey said. "Hey, Bill! Which ones are the easier questions?"

"Tell me about it," said Estella.

"But golf balls are little," Dacey said. "I can't believe they even have a hundred dimples. It has to be number two."

Jig let out a laugh. "And your fact-based reference is . . ."

"Fine. If no one else has anything, move on."

QUESTION #4

HOW MANY SPECIES OF FLIGHTLESS BIRDS CURRENTLY EXIST?

CHOOSE 1 IF THAT ANSWER IS EQUAL TO OR GREATER THAN 4.

CHOOSE 2 IF THAT ANSWER IS LESS THAN 4.

"Okay," said Clio. "There's the ostrich and emu. Also penguins."

"What about the ones that look like penguins?" said Jig. "Puffins?"

"They fly," said Clio. "That's one of the differences."

"Really?" said Dacey. "And you know this because . . ."

"My kindergarten teacher was obsessed with penguins. But what's important, I think there are more flightless birds in Australia, and two more would make five. But I'm like Cameron with the decibels, only ninety percent sure."

They moved on.

QUESTION #5

WHEN WAS THE FIRST JUNGLE GYM BUILT?

CHOOSE 1 IF THAT ANSWER IS BEFORE GOLLY TOY AND GAME COMPANY WAS ESTABLISHED.

CHOOSE 2 IF THAT ANSWER IS AFTER GOLLY TOY AND GAME COMPANY WAS ESTABLISHED.

"Got it!" Dacey said. "If you don't know, you don't deserve to be here. This is Golly's fifty-first anniversary."

"So before or after fifty-one years ago?" Jig said.

"Oops," said Dacey. "Not sure."

"I might be, though," said Clio. "My grandma has this story about getting over her fear of heights on a jungle gym, and she's, well, I think she's over sixty years old."

"And we have nothing definitive," said Jig.

"All we can do is use our closest guesses." Clio pulled paper and a pen from her pocket. "More or less than eighteen glacier countries?"

Cameron, Jig, and Estella voted more; Dacey and Clio, less.

"Majority rules for now," Clio said, writing down a 1. "But the underlining means we're not unanimous. More or less than eighty-five decibels?"

They were unanimous. She marked down the 2.

"More or less than two hundred golf ball dimples?"

Split decision, boys versus girls. She underlined the 2, for less.

"More or less than four flightless birds?"

More. Unanimous. She wrote the 1.

"Jungle gym. Before Golly or after."

Before. Unanimous again. Another 1 on the paper.

"Let's see what matches up best," she said.

They ran back to the doors, with their choices.

First door: 1 2 1 1 1

Second door: 2 2 1 1 2

Third door: 1 1 2 2 1

* * * *

They compared those with their paper: <u>1</u> 2 <u>2</u> 1 1

"If you look at the ones we're unanimous on," said Clio, "it's the first door."

"We can't be sure, can we?" said Dacey.

"What's the question we feel most confident about?" said Clio. "Jungle gym?"

They agreed.

"So we'll eliminate door number two."

"If we do," said Jig, "majority was right on the glacier question because the remaining doors are both choice number one."

Silence. Cameron was more than ninety percent on the decibels, but what if he was wrong?

"Hey!" said Dacey. "Weren't we supposed to get a hint? Where's the puzzle card?"

There was still nothing on the back.

"Wait!" Cameron pulled the packet of lemon juice from his pocket and ripped it open with his teeth, spraying half of it on his shirt. He sprinkled the rest onto the back of the card and spread it with his fingers. Letters started appearing: *Cas* . . . But he didn't have enough juice to reveal any others.

"Genius!" Clio said.

She and Estella pulled out their packets and spread more juice over the card. It finished the first word—*Cassowary*—and started the next, *Ki*. "Two birds, I think. More juice!"

Jig rubbed his to the end of the first line, then underneath from the right.

Cassowary Kiwi

s   l

Jig held the card out. "Get the rest of that line, Dacey."

She looked down. "Weren't y'all worried the packet might burst on your clothes?"

"Perfect," said Estella.

"We're okay," Clio said. "We can go with what we have. The new birds make at least five, so fourth position is a one. Eliminates door number three. It's door number one, Dacey."

She grabbed the knob. "Y'all sure?"

"It's on me if this is wrong," said Clio. "Open it!"

It opened into the Rainbow Maze.

"If we messed up," said Jig, "you won't regret it."

The stunt card was attached to the yellow wall.

Stunt #5

* * * * * * * * * * *

WELCOME TO THE RAINBOW MAZE!

Weave in and out, and in and out.

It's last year's maze, there is no doubt.

But now, of all the paths you choose—

The reds, the oranges, greens, and blues—

You'll find no reason or no rhyme.

Dead ends will show you're wrong this time.

And stick together every turn

Or penalties will be quite stern.

Instead of sticks along your way,

You need to find four packs today.

Each of you must bring your four

Up to the very highest door.

And then . . .

"And then," said Jig, "the most amazing slide. You can't even imagine."

Or not. Things were different this year, but Cameron wasn't going to argue, not when he was in the middle of magic. For the first time ever he was happier without his camera. Nothing could capture the amazing radiance of all these colors showering down on them.

They climbed a set of purple stairs that led to their first choice—right, left, or straight. Jig was the fastest runner, and last year Rocky had come in first by running, so . . .

Jig turned right into the orange passageway without asking. No one said anything. This was a good strategy. No debating. No words, just—

Dead end. They turned around; Jig pushed to the front and led them straight to the green, up a long ramp that curved to a choice of yellow or blue hallways. Jig ran to the blue. Up ten stairs. Right to green and—

"Stop!" Cameron called from the third position in line behind Jig.

Clio turned. "Jig! Jig! Come back."

He did.

Cameron grabbed five small tape-sealed gear bags

that were lying in a shadow on the ground. "I don't think we're supposed to open these." He slung one over his shoulder and handed the rest out.

"At least we know we're right so far," said Dacey.

But other than that, even she was quiet. All the stairs, all the uphill running took a lot of breath, and they were only getting started.

Up through orange, which morphed into red and came to a dead end. Down and back to a deep blue, then up to red, left to yellow, and even Jig saw them: their second packs.

Halfway done with those. Unless. His stomach lurched. What if they'd been so hypnotized by the colors they'd missed one? What if they had to go all the way back?

He had to wipe away the thought because panic would pull too much breath from his lungs. Instead, he tried to memorize the color order in case they needed to double back.

But they'd gone left at purple, right at green and had to return to go up red instead, and now up more green stairs and up a spiral yellow ramp. No way to remember.

"Gear bags!" Jig called.

Pack number three sat in a blue hall that spoked four different ways. Jig picked purple, but after four stairs and a short passageway, dead end. Back to red. Up fourteen steps, which had them all panting. The red morphed into purple, then into blue that led up and up.

Even Jig was slowing down. Thank goodness. The packs weren't that heavy alone, but combined, they had some heft. As Cameron ran, the rope drawstrings dug further into his shoulders and the lumpy contents slapped at his back.

How many steps had they climbed? How many up ramps had they run? Next, a green straightaway. Then blue stairs. Red stairs. Yellow ramp. Orange stairs. Green straightaway. Some dead ends, some through passages.

They made a big sweeping red curve and came foot-to-foot with their last pack and face-to-face with six doors, one red, one orange, one yellow, one green, one blue, and one purple.

"Thank . . . heavens." Dacey leaned over, hands on thighs, and gasped for air.

"Instructions say we have to bring the pack to the very highest door," said Estella, who'd apparently thought to bring the stunt card. "And none of these look higher than the others."

"I bet they shove a penalty at us if we open the wrong one," said Dacey.

"Nothing about that in the instructions." Jig pulled open the red door to a solid brick wall.

It was the blue for the Blue Team. Cameron knew it, but they wouldn't be certain until they'd compared everything.

Estella opened the orange and leaned in. "Just three steps, then another dead end."

"One of them has to go up more," said Clio. "Everyone, open a door, but just look in. Remember, we have to stay together."

Cameron pulled open the blue and leaned way in. Three stairs went up to a landing that seemed to continue to the right.

"Yellow's a dead end," called Estella.

"So's green," said Jig.

"Blue keeps going," said Cameron.

"So does purple. C'mon." Clio led them up five

stairs, down a short purple hall to another door, a higher door. She opened it to what looked like a dead-end room. "Go in? Or try blue?"

"Blue," said Cameron. "We're the Blue Team."

Out through purple, in through blue, up three steps, hairpin curve right, around a hotel-length hall, sharp left, up a ramp. Definitely higher than purple. The flight of rainbow-lit stairs rose to a large darkened room that ended with a golden door. The highest door, no question.

Estella reached for it. The door went dark. "Ahh!"

"What?"

"Who?"

A mass of people streamed in, dressed, as far as Cameron could tell, in black, skintight clothes from hoods on down. And what was over their eyes? Night vision goggles?

"No worries," came Bill's voice. "They're here to help. Let them."

The four people around Cameron grabbed his packs and opened them. One sat him in a chair while another put a helmet on his head; yet another, gloves on his hands. The fourth person was shoving straps or something over his feet. "Stand and pull them up," the person said.

Cameron did. He felt hands buckling him into what felt like a harness. Someone handed him a bar. They moved him forward, and the gold door gradually lit until it glowed. Cameron was in line behind Estella and Clio. Shortest to tallest?

Only two people flanked each of them now. They guided the five of them by the elbows through the golden door and onto a platform. They stopped.

This year there was no slide. The Rainbow Maze was open all around them. Above them, cables and pulleys.

Within ten seconds the people had them hooked to a zip line. The platform below them dropped.

"Aah!"

Cameron's stomach spent only an instant in his throat before the rush took over, the wind stinging his eyes, blowing back his hair, whooshing past his ears. He was flying! Soaring! At breakneck speed!

He dared to look around at the whizzing blur of the mountain, the sunflowers, the elephant, jack-o'-lanterns, three-story birthday cake. They dipped down, down, down—

Oof! Into a tight curve. Then the zip line seemed to lift them higher only to quick-fall some more. Around and around and—

Would they let him do this again? And again? The feeling. The colors. The ground. The ground? Too soon, way too soon, there was the ground. How would they slow down? How would they stop?

But the ground opened. They were going below. To the losers' dungeon?

Suddenly, abruptly, they slowed. The line had mostly leveled out. They soared slowly at first, then faster and faster on a line that remained level about ten feet from the ground. It had to be powered somehow.

"Whee!" yelled Dacey.

"Who needs the slide?" said Jig.

Cameron just grinned. But where was this taking them? Were they out? Ejected? On the street? Or maybe, possibly, had they made up the time they needed? Should he even dare to hope?

They slowed again. The area grew darker and darker, then pitch-black. Bodies fussed around him to the sound of clicking and unclicking, then whirring and hissing.

"Huh?"

A seat moved in under him. A roller-coaster-type bar clamped down on his lap.

The whirring and hissing continued, and the room began lighting from above. The roof was opening, and they were sitting in individual baskets of mini hot-air balloons. The balloons started rising and rising and rising until they were soaring over the armor, over the peacocks, over the pigs, over the nose, over everything in the puzzle-stunt room.

"Yes!" Cameron shouted.

No one, though, had said they'd won.

CHAPTER 24

Could that have been a losers' treat? Was the Orange Team already celebrating to the tune of horns, the shower of confetti? Were they dancing around a sign that flashed WINNERS!

The sign! The horns! The confetti! It was theirs!

A platform slid underneath them. The people in the skintight suits released them from their balloons. Off with the helmets. Off with the gloves. Off with the zip-line harnesses.

On with the jumping and screaming and shouting! On with the dancing and hugging. In with Bill, throwing aside a mop and a broom and a feather duster. He ran in circles. He turned a cartwheel.

"You did it! I didn't think it was possible. I lied. You were more than six minutes behind. I didn't want you to freak out and, and yet they were still debating flightless birds when you picked up your first packs. They never did remember the lemon juice."

Bill gathered them in a huddle. He put an arm around Cameron and stuck his other arm in the middle. The hands piled up. "So this is how it is to win. I couldn't be prouder. Blue Team on three," he said. "One, two, three . . ."

"Blue Team," they all yelled, and broke huddle.

More jumping, more shouting, more dancing, and then Jig dropped to the floor and put his head in his hands.

Cameron had almost hit the celebration wall, too. Half of him wanted to continue, but the other half needed a bed.

They all collapsed on the ground.

"Anything you want to know?" Bill said.

Probably, but Cameron's brain had switched off.

"Those questions?" asked Dacey. "Exactly which three were easy?"

Bill smiled. "It wasn't the questions themselves,"

he said. "It was your choices. The Orange Team won only two of the head-to-heads, so their cutoff number for flightless birds wasn't four. Theirs was eight. And we could have given you seventy decibels and three hundred golf ball dimples. Who'd think they could fit between three and five hundred dimples on something that small? But they do."

"And glaciers?" asked Estella.

"Forty-seven countries. Sixty decibels in normal conversation. About forty species of flightless birds. And the first documented jungle gym appeared in 1920. The harder version of that had you guessing before or after 1899."

A set of doors slid open. Cameron struggled up with the others. In came four of the only five people who could understand what they were feeling—Gil, Bianca, Lavinia, and Thorn.

No way Bianca would remember him, but she broke free of the pack, walked right up, and gave him a hug. "Cameron! I told you!" She turned to the others. "I had a feeling about him at his regional. I was so right! How are you? All excited and exhausted with mush for brains that want to explode and celebrate at the same time? Well, probably not you. You're smarter than me. I watched. We all watched." She leaned over and whispered, "If it weren't for you, well, you and Clio, the three of them would still be arguing." She straightened. "And look at me. I'm hogging you. Come meet my friends."

This was a different Gil from the one last year on TV. This Gil was taller, and he looked more confident. If only the Games could give Cameron that, too. Not the taller—he'd get that eventually—but the confidence. Maybe he'd already grown some. It was going to take a chisel to knock the grin from his face.

Lavinia, last year's runner-up, gave him a hug. She looked more relaxed than Cameron remembered. "Bianca must really like you," she said. "The whole time, she told us to watch you. How did you impress her so much?"

Cameron shook his head. "I barely said anything. You can't exactly talk a lot around her."

Lavinia laughed. "You just proved my theory."

Thorn joined them. "What theory? About the strong, silent types?"

"That," Lavinia said, "and chemistry, too. I think Cameron is——"

Bill came up to them. "Wait till you see lunch. Hope you're hungry, Cameron."

Hungry? He was hungry for Lavinia to finish that last sentence. Cameron is what?

Too late. The conversation dropped. Well, mostly. Jig was still trying to hang all over Bianca, and even though she was smiling and talking, she was also leaning away. Bill casually came between the two of them, thumped Jig on the back, and let Bianca make her escape to join Clio as they walked down a hallway.

If he'd had his camera, Cameron would have zoomed in on Bill's hand, keeping Jig from doubling back for Bianca. He'd have taken some frames of Lavinia's bouncing hair and edited that against the stiff ponytail she had last year. He'd have shot Thorn's feet where his expensive shoes met the frayed hem of his jeans. And Gil? Where was he?

Cameron glanced around to his right but felt someone come up on his left.

"So you're Bianca's favorite?" he said.

Cameron felt his head start to sweat even more. "I don't know."

"It's a good thing," said Gil. "I was. She tells me all the time." He laughed. "What did you think when your brother showed up?"

"That I wished he'd go away."

Gil pointed they'd be turning right down the next hallway. "You can blame me for that."

"Why?"

"Last year I made some comment about having an unfair disadvantage, that no one else had his worst nightmare dogging him every step of the way."

"You said that?" Cameron would have remembered.

"Probably a boring version of that so it didn't make TV. But one of the Golly people heard me and thought, Oh, wouldn't it be fun to make all the contestants as crazy as Rocky made Gil."

"And he's here again."

"No big deal. I'm past that. But you have to deal with Spencer every day."

Cameron nodded. "If I'd been competing against anyone else, I probably wouldn't have blown it."

Gil had them turn down a short hallway with an

open door and food smells coming straight at them. "You didn't blow anything. You're here, right?" Gil slowed and let Cameron through the door first.

Before he could get his second foot in, Walker pounced on him from the side. "Do you know who that was? Do you know who you were talking to?"

Before he could answer, his parents were all over him with the we're-so-proud thing and the you-were-so-good thing, and he actually believed them because—

It hit him. Cameron really was one of the final five; everyone would watch him this year. And even with all the hugging and holding on, he felt his knees buckle for a second. He couldn't freak out now. He had to keep going. He had to stop thinking.

"Where's the food?" he said.

"Food? What food?" His mom took him by the shoulders and spun him around.

He zeroed in on the trio of chocolate volcanoes— dark chocolate, milk chocolate, and white chocolate. He wanted to run his hand along them all, then lick it off. Behind them, well, he'd never seen so much food in his life.

"Just like last year," said Gil, coming up from behind. "One tip: Choose wisely. You don't want a food coma for the next round. And they'll have it out for you again afterward." He patted him on the back. "Time for me to see Rocky."

Walker grabbed his arm. "That was him again! That was Gil!"

Cameron laughed. "What are you going to eat?"

"Everything," Walker said. "Unless Spencer eats it all first."

Where was Spencer? Probably looking for Bianca again, but no. He wasn't with her. He was alone in the food line. Cameron went up to him. "What looks good?"

Spencer stabbed a fat hamburger and put it on his plate. "Pretty much everything." He added some chicken fingers and a mound of potato salad.

"What's the deal?" said Cameron. "You beat me

in Who's There? You were the first one done. You looked like you were back in Spencer mode, having fun even."

"I was in the heat of competition. Got a taste of what could've been. Not so much now. Just run along and play."

Cameron stepped back and got a plate. He turned toward another food table but walked up to Spencer instead. "You know," he said, his heart beating nearly as fast as on the Rainbow Maze, "I didn't sign up for this, and I didn't cheat you out of a spot. If it wasn't me here, it still wouldn't be you."

Spencer took Cameron's plate for himself and added some barbecued brisket and a bun. He moved to the next table and grabbed a handful of cookies. "You don't have to remind me. And you definitely don't need to baby me like Mom and Dad. Let me sulk for five minutes, and I'll be fine."

"Yeah. You will be." Cameron was tempted to find Bianca to cheer him up, but it wouldn't hurt Spencer to feel this way for a while. Cameron had pretty much felt it for his whole life. Not anymore. Well, probably not. Well, maybe sometimes. But not today.

He got two plates he would keep this time.

His dad came up and ruffled his hair again. "Hey, champ! Is Spencer okay?"

Really? Cameron's reign as Kid for a Day was over? "He just needs a few minutes." So did Cameron. "I'm going to the pizza table. They have your favorite over there, fried chicken."

Cameron didn't really want pizza. He wanted to get away. But pizza was always good. He took a piece loaded with hamburger. Then he took some egg rolls and a taco and had a world culture thing going with his two plates.

Spencer was at a round table by himself. Cameron sat two chairs away. He took a bite, then realized their whole family would be there in a minute. "How much did they give you?"

Spencer barely looked up. "A thousand bucks for showing up. Three thousand more for beating you." He lifted his head. "Then, because two of us won, we split another pot of five thousand dollars. So five thousand in all. If those other three doofuses had kicked it, we would have split twenty-five thousand dollars instead."

"Not a bad day's work."

Spencer laughed. "Not at all."

"You know I didn't sign my name on the contract."

"What contract?"

Was he kidding? "The one where we split things fifty-fifty?"

"So?"

"You already got some money, maybe even more than I'll get."

Spencer shrugged. "Your point?"

"I'm keeping what I win." There, he'd said it. "I'm not splitting anything."

"You didn't seriously think I could make you."

Cameron shrugged.

Spencer gave him a shove and returned to sulk mode in time for their mom and dad and Walker to see.

Between bites, his parents recapped the action. The gushing was good at first, but then it became like too much chocolate cake, losing its specialness after two huge slices.

Chocolate. He hadn't had that yet. He went over to the volcanoes. Golly even had individual spigots rigged up, so he could stick his fingers under running chocolate without recirculating contaminated lava.

He took a swipe of the dark chocolate, then washed it down with the milk chocolate. The plan was to end with the white chocolate, but Spencer came up and stuck his finger under there. Cameron stuck his finger underneath, too.

A food service person ran up. "You can't share. We have food safety laws against that."

"He's my brother," said Spencer. "It's what we do."

They licked their fingers, and the food service guy backed off.

"So I'm looking at your competition." Spencer stared at the volcano. "Unless a series of freak sunspots blind you, you're in the top three. Dacey has no chance. Her person, Laura Ramirez, told me she freezes when it gets tough."

"She obviously didn't freeze in the stadium. She's here."

Spencer took another swipe of chocolate. "I just know what Laura told me. When Dacey flubbed up at pageants, she'd accuse Laura of being lazy and paying off the judges. And Laura would smile and drive Dacey crazy. Don't worry about Estella, either. She might be good, but she's still in meltdown over that ex-boyfriend. When we were waiting, Stephen said she was going to freak out, but I have to give her credit. She whipped him."

"Where is he?"

"With the losing team. He was so mad he couldn't get in her face right now."

"Good guy, huh?"

"He was actually pretty funny, but I'm glad I'm not her. You've gotta watch out for Jig, though. He's like Rocky was last year. Rocky told me so himself. Don't trust the guy."

"What will he do?"

"Talk smack. Try to psych you out. Did you notice when he was basically doing nothing? That was on purpose. He once told Rocky that if he ever got in the Games, he'd let his team fall behind, then come save the day and be the TV hero."

Cameron nodded. "Clio figured that out. So, did he look like the hero?"

Spencer shook his head no. "It was a toss-up."

"Between Clio and who?"

Spencer shoved him in the shoulder, turned, and walked away.

Lunch Following the
TEAM COMPETITION

"This can't be good," said Larraine from Finance.

"You think?" said Bert Golliwop. "We're supposed to be whooping it up with the winners, and instead, we're in an empty conference room. No food, no fun."

Jenkins from Human Resources was the last in the room. "Now what?" she said. "It's not another one of my people out with the flu, is it? Who gets the flu in August?"

"I don't know if it's one of your people," said Burt, head in his hands. "But you should know what it is. You all should know. Who in tarnation broadcast privileged information on every live computer screen in the building?" He looked up. "We need to know, and know now: Where were our contestants during those five minutes?"

"Do you want me to get Carol and Bill?" Jenkins asked.

"I've already talked to all the escorts," said Tawkler from Marketing. "The whereabouts of every contestant is accounted for during that time."

"At least there's that," said Bert. "At least we don't need to switch to an alternate challenge."

There was a brief tap on the door before it opened. Danny, the intern, handed Bert a sheet of paper, then left.

Bert scanned the paper, then put it down. "Our airtight system was hacked. And my question is, Why can't the genius who did that work for me and not for Flummox?"

Morrison from Legal cleared his throat. "We can't assume it's Flummox, Bert. You realize it might be some random, crazy person out for notoriety or trying to make a buck."

"Yes," said Jenkins. "And I can't see the people at Flummox—"

"You dare stand up for my competitor, Jenkins? I thought you worked for me."

Jenkins paled. "I-I do, sir. It's just—"

Bert Golliwop held up a hand. "Forget it, Jenkins. You stand up for your employees every day. That's in your nature and why you're good."

The red raced back to her cheeks. "That's very kind—"

"But I still doubt it's someone out for a buck. If that were true, they'd hold our information for ransom instead of trying to sabotage us. And who might want to sabotage us? That dirty, rotten, cheating—" He took in a breath because finger-pointing wouldn't help. And if it was Flummox, with his ingenious puzzle division, it would be hard to prove.

"Be careful," Morrison said. "With such limited thinking, we may be targeting an innocent suspect, therefore overlooking the real criminal."

"Yes!" said Jenkins. "It may not even be within our industry. Though I could have sworn I did catch a glimpse of Flummox in that rat-infested arena. I'll bet—"

"Seriously, Jenkins?" said Tawkler from Marketing. "You may be great managing this whole employee system, but you'd flunk as a spy. If it is Flummox, it's not likely he'd show his face. He'd pay someone working here to carry out his plans."

"I knew that," said Jenkins. "I just wasn't, um—maybe the flu is getting to me."

"The bottom line is this," said Bert. "We need to flush out the mole, whoever he or she is."

"Excuse me." Jenkins pointed to the paper under Bert's hands. "What about Danny? He's been sitting in on meetings. I didn't clear him. I didn't even hire him. How'd that happen?"

"I hired him," said Bert, "and it's not Danny."

"How do you know?" said Jenkins.

"I've known his family forever. I also know he could have gone to grad school at Harvard or Brown, but I insisted he come here to get both classroom and practical education."

"College kids are notoriously poor. Maybe he needed the money."

"This isn't about that, Jenkins. This is about jealousy and corporate greed. But there's nothing else we can do now. Let's go meet the kids and eat something."

"Even so," Bert heard Jenkins whisper to Larraine on their way out, "it wouldn't hurt to keep our eyes on the intern."

CHAPTER 25

After lunch, Bill led them through a series of winding halls into a large room. "Even Jig didn't see our lounge last year. Except for us monitoring you, this space is totally private. No public cameras or microphones unless we tell you. You have full access to me if you need it. Just push this." He motioned to a green, plate-sized button on the wall. "Try it, Dacey."

She pressed it with one finger.

"No," said Bill. "Really pound it with your fist."

She gave it a whack, and the room went dark. Eerie music came up.

Bill banged the button, and the room returned to normal. He stopped laughing and spoke into his headset. "Thanks, Danny. That was fun." He swiveled the microphone away from his mouth. "Sorry. My lame attempt at humor. There is no magic button. Nothing brings the lights down or the music up unless you have Danny in the control room working the joke. If you need me, yell. If you're still hungry, eat."

One part of the room looked like it came straight from a convenience store. It had a four-flavor ice cream machine, shelves of sweet and salty snacks, and a drink dispenser with fifteen types of soda and lemonade. Bill pointed out the bathrooms, then directed them to the five large armchairs in the middle of the lounge, each with noise-canceling headphones and a touch screen monitor with a huge menu of videos, games, music, books, and magazines.

They stood there like a tour group. "We have a few more details to take care of," said Bill, "before we send you onward."

A man in a dark suit and toy-printed tie walked in like he owned the place. Actually, he did own the place. It was Mr. Golliwop. "I've just come from con-gratulating your opponents for their fine efforts. And you five! What great assets to our Games! You've all played honorably. I expect that to continue."

Mr. Golliwop gestured toward Jig. "This young man knows how disappointing it is to have that window of opportunity close on him. Though heaven knows what you were thinking, Mr. Jiggerson, in naming your competitor. It's been quite awkward bringing him back. Be that as it may, we fully anticipate you all will continue to be models of integrity and intelligence from here on out.

"And now that I've given my boring little speech, please take your chairs and pay attention to your monitors."

Cameron settled into the most comfortable chair ever. It hugged him without making him feel he'd suffocate. His monitor showed the Orange Team in a colorful conference room with five large trunks. The camera panned to five more trunks on the other side of the room.

"No matter what happens," said Mr. Golliwop, "you'll each receive one of those. And some of this—"

The feed cut to one kid fanning himself with a wad of hundred-dollar bills.

"How much is that?" Jig asked.

Mr. Golliwop smiled. "Enough for now. Also inside your trunks is our newest GollyGamer, which won't come out for months. And of course there's another thing or two you might find interesting."

Like last year, when they'd hidden an important puzzle piece in the trunk? Wasn't anyone going to ask? He wasn't. No reason to tip off the competition. Anyway, how would he ever find that room if he needed it?

Cameron brushed the hair from his eyes. He was overthinking again. New rule: If he had no other options, he'd figure out where it was. The end.

Their screens went dark. "Relax," said Bill. "I'll be back soon." He left with Mr. Golliwop.

Dacey leaned over to Cameron. "So, your brother. He's a little doll. Or a big one."

Cameron's brother wasn't any doll. "Spencer's the reason I'm here. He—"

"Sweet," said Dacey, apparently uninterested in the rest of the story. She leaned over to Jig.

"Your friend," Jig said before Dacey could say anything. "She's a little doll. Or a tall one."

"She's a ditz," said Dacey. "She always managed to cheat or something to win the pageants. That's why I quit. I swear they were rigged. But you," she said to Jig, "you had the audacity to bring back Rocky."

"If I'd known, I would've asked for my dumb little sister."

"I would have kept Janae," said Clio. "She's the fiercest person I know."

They all looked at Estella. "Never in a million years," she said. "They asked who I wouldn't want, and his ugly, cheating face flashed before my eyes."

"At least they sent him away for lunch," said Dacey, "and you had those people around you."

"My family," said Estella. "My mom and dad and my little brother and sister. They're a pain, especially when they don't listen to me, but they have my back."

"And you have theirs," said Clio.

Estella nodded, then shook her head. "What if they bring the jerk back?"

"Just pretend every step you take pushes a voodoo pin into him," said Clio.

Estella almost smiled. "If you don't mind, I'm going to turn my chair around and breathe for a minute." She tiptoed with her feet until the back of her chair faced them.

"Too bad she'll miss out on my secret," said Jig. "I wasn't going to say anything, but it wouldn't be fair if only I knew this." He leaned in toward them. "You know what Mr. Golliwop was hinting at with those trunks, don't you?"

"What?" said Dacey.

"When the time comes, think about how they needed them last year."

"Right," said Dacey.

Jig nodded. "And one more thing. Remember when Gil dropped his sticks last year? It wasn't because of Rocky. It was the pressure of needing the money. Gil was wiping sweat off his palms the whole time." He rubbed his hands together. "Ever since then I swear I've been training my hands not to sweat, and it works. All you do is concentrate on the part affected by stress."

Dacey was rubbing her nose. "It itches when I get nervous. I've seen videos of me twitching like a bunny."

"You see?" said Jig. "Tell it not to itch. Or concentrate on your ears instead."

She looked sideways like she was trying to see her ear. "It helped!" But then she rubbed her nose. "Well, almost."

Cameron touched the top of his head. It was starting to sweat again. He'd barely felt it all day. Maybe he'd been too busy to notice. Maybe now that he was relaxing—

Seriously? He was falling for it. Spencer was right. Jig was trying to psych them out.

Clio rolled her eyes. She motioned for Cameron to turn his chair around. She came over and knelt by him. "You know what he's trying to do."

Cameron nodded. "My brother warned me he would."

"Don't listen," she said.

"You, either."

The door burst open, pretty much scaring the wits out of Cameron. Bill was back. "Who's ready to play more Games?"

Cameron sucked in a deep breath.

CHAPTER 26

"Sit back!" Bill said.

"We're competing in chairs?" asked Jig.

"Nope."

"Thank goodness," Estella said. "I could fall asleep here. Best chair ever."

"And you get to keep it!" said Bill. "Parting gift with the trunk and whatever."

"Hey!" said Jig. "What's going on?"

The lounge was moving.

"Why walk when you can ride?" Bill put a hand on Jig's chair back. "We're heading to five separate challenge rooms. There you'll be on your own," he said. "If you have an emergency (and I'm talking bleeding or worse), yell. But if you need to scream in frustration, yell, 'I'm frustrated!' This whole competition works best when we adults can sit in the background, eating our chocolate and sipping our coffee."

The lounge came to a stop.

"Let's do this!"

They stepped out the lounge door and into a cozy, round area. Its windows, though, must have had video screens instead of glass because they showed sandy shores with crashing waves.

"Our little attempt at humor in the Midwest." Bill positioned them each in front of a door. "When you hear the signal, go!"

Cameron hoped he could hear the signal over his thumping heart. He shouldn't have worried. Waves crashed. His door opened. He rushed in. The door clicked shut behind him.

Four more doors lined the wall ahead. All locked. On the desk behind him sat a clear container just smaller than a basketball net. It was about a quarter filled with keys. At the three-quarter mark was a tube feeding in more keys, a few at a time.

Next to it was a flexible plastic card, larger than any stunt or puzzle card by far.

In puzzles like these
You find the right keys.
You open the doors.
You look at the floors.
Four things belong;
Four others are wrong.
BUT (AND HERE COME THE RULES)
Select just one key—
Not two and not three.
Then try it before
You go back for more.
OH. AND . . .
To make it more tough
(It's not hard enough),
The person you know
Will make your task grow.
(They're all unaware
What they're doing up there.)
TURN ON THE MONITOR ABOVE THE DESK.
* * * *

Not again! On the screen, Spencer and Rocky and Laura and Stephen and Janae were picking up three keys on one side of a room and depositing them in one of five tubes on the other. Worse, Spencer and Rocky were moving as if they were in a race for a billion dollars.

Cameron had to hurry before Spencer made his entire container spill over. He grabbed the first key he touched and tried it in the first lock. It didn't fit, not even past the tip. It swam in the second lock. It got partway into the third. And no go in the fourth. He ran back and put the key inside an empty container he assumed was for discards. He grabbed another key. This was definitely not your normal door key. The part you stuck in the lock was square and hollow.

He ran it over and looked at the keyholes. The first door's keyhole was smaller than normal. The second's was square like the key he was holding. He tried it. It went in perfectly but didn't turn. The third's was like the ones at his house. The keyhole on the fourth was larger with space for two sets of notches, one on the top and one on the bottom.

This was good. He'd only need to try each key in one lock. Next key. Square. Door number two. No. Next. Large and notched on two sides. Door four. No luck. Normal key. Door three. No. Very long, very skinny key. Door one. No.

He glanced at the screen. Spencer was still racing with all his might. Poor Estella was probably transfixed by her old boyfriend. And why was he worried about Estella now?

More keys. He tried two normal ones. Another square one. A skinny one. Three two-sided ones. Another square one, and yes! Door two.

Inside was nothing but a small closet space with a couple of toys on the floor. Those would have to wait. Right now it was a race against all those keys Spencer was sending down the chute.

New game plan. He rooted through the container for normal-looking keys. They'd get buried more easily and be harder to find. If only he could stop the new ones from coming!

He tried the first normal key in door number three. No. Second key. No. Third. No. By the time he went back for a fourth key, he had to dig to find one beneath a barrage of new square keys, which he didn't need.

The keys were almost as high as the feeding tube. Spencer was still running. Hard. Fast. If only he'd trip and give Cameron a break. If only Cameron could take off his shirt and stuff it in the feed tube. Wait. Not a bad idea. Unless there was a rule against it. But being half naked on national TV? No, but—

Maybe his instruction card was large and flexible for a reason. He held it inside the container, against the feed tube with one hand. With the other, he clawed a bunch of keys against the card to hold it into place.

Spencer dropped in three more keys. The card held! The keys were staying in the tube!

Back to normal keys. He tried four more until

the fifth worked. Door number three, open. He couldn't help himself. On the floor were both the zipper and shoelace cards from the old Dress Me, Dress You learning game. In the other door were the GollyRocket and GollyCopter. And these were supposed to have something in common?

He'd been better off knowing nothing. Spencer was still rushing over with the keys, and no telling how long the card would hold. Unless . . .

Oh, no! What if Spencer was feeding him keys he needed? Forget that for now. He could always reopen the floodgate later. Cameron grabbed a double-notched key. Why couldn't the first one work on door number four? Or the second? Why did it take eight of them?

Cameron knew better than to glance toward this floor, but it was like roadkill; he had to see. Two new objects: GollyGlitter and GollyGlue.

Back to the container. The card was leaning in like a dam about to burst. He shoved more keys against it, but they would hold only for a while. He had to get the last door open.

Time for the long, skinny keys. One, two, three.

No, no, no. Four, five, six. No, no, no. Seven, eight, nine, ten. Eleven!

He pulled out the staircase and wardrobe from Mystery at Golly Mansion. He brought over the rest of the objects and laid them on the desk. What was he supposed to do now? He pulled the card from the container to a key avalanche. "Four things belong, four others are wrong."

"It's wrong they don't give us another hint," he muttered.

But they'd given him a drawer in the desk! False alarm. It had paper and pens and nothing. He used them, though, to list what he had:

Shoelace

Zipper

Wardrobe

Stairs

Glue

Glitter

Rocket

Helicopter

* * * *

Step one, process of elimination. It couldn't be the words themselves because Golly hadn't instructed him to call it a helicopter or copter or chopper; a lace or a shoelace; steps or stairs. It had to be the objects themselves, not their names.

So what did four have in common? Similar markings? Nope. Common objects versus not? His house had stairs, glue, shoelaces, zippers; but Dacey probably had glitter, and Golly couldn't have predicted who owned what.

Next idea. The colors? The dates Golly introduced the products? What the company still made and what it didn't? No, no, and no. The answer had to be simple. Right now his brain was completely blank. And even when he figured this out, what was he supposed to do with the four things that belonged?

He inspected inside and underneath the desk drawer for writing. Nothing. Hoping the screen had more info now, he touched the monitor. Spencer and the rest were still running for keys. Not for long, though. The key wall was mostly empty.

So was the rest of Cameron's room. Nothing else inside the closets. Nothing under the desk. Just the key container, discard container, monitor—

Back up. He dumped out the keys from the discard container. At the very bottom it said, "Deposit the four that belong in here. Close the other four inside any of the closets."

Yes! Back to the puzzle. Fresh brain. Fresh ideas. What fresh ideas? Maybe if he focused on the objects one at a time . . .

You tie a shoelace. You zip a zipper. You put clothes into a wardrobe. Shoes? Zipper? Wardrobe? What else has to do with getting dressed? Nothing. Unless he used glue and glitter to make a shirt. And no.

Still, he liked his direction. You tie a shoelace. You put clothes in a wardrobe. Or you open a wardrobe. Were there other things that opened? Not really. Onward. You stick things together with glue. A rocket flies. So does a helicopter. They lift up. They come down. And the stairs! You go up and down a staircase. One more thing.

Cameron scanned the objects, grabbed the zipper, zipped it down, then up!

He put the up-and-down things into the container. He threw the shoelace card, the glitter, the glue, and the wardrobe onto the floor of the second door and slammed it shut.

Now what? Nothing on the monitor. But the discard container suddenly glowed. It lifted up, up, up toward the ceiling. Cameron started looking for a trick wire, but the entry door opened.

Bill thumped him on the back. "Good work!"

"Fast enough?"

Bill pointed to their lounge. "See for yourself."

CHAPTER 27

Clio was the only one in the room. She sipped from her glass, then smiled at him. "I'm glad it's you."

"Me, too." He took a deep breath. "I mean that it's you."

"So what did you think was harder, Cameron? Keys or objects?"

He hadn't sorted it all out yet. "Equal, I guess. What about you?"

"The objects. I mean, you did stop the keys, didn't you? Slid the card into the grooves?"

"What grooves?"

"The two grooves at the top of the key bin," said Clio. "They held the card in place."

"I just wedged it in there."

"That works, too."

Maybe, but Cameron was kicking himself. He always noticed little things like that. Was he getting lazy without his camera? He got a glass of lemonade, sat, and sighed.

"I know," she said. "It's like an endurance test. I wouldn't give this up for anything, but it'd be even better if we could go home and eat dinner and sleep between each event."

"Yeah," said Cameron. "Well, no. I'd be obsessing over it so much I wouldn't sleep, my brain would overheat, and I'd be a pile of ashes in the morning."

Clio smiled. "You did okay from yesterday to today."

He nodded; then they sat there in comfortable silence until the door opened.

Jig barged in like he owned the place. He tried to look all cool when he saw them, but his slight pause gave him away. Maybe Cameron could still notice details.

"That was a bear," Jig said. "Not the up-and-down thing—that was easy—but those keys! Rocky was relentless. How'd you get here before me, Cameron?"

"Just lucky, I guess." No way he'd give Jig any tips.

"Who got in here first?"

"I did," Clio said.

"Thought so. Your girl wasn't as fast as our guys."

"True." That's all Clio said. She leaned back in her chair and closed her eyes.

The silence didn't last long. The door opened. It was Estella, beaming. "I did it! I forgot that pig was there and just did it." She gave Clio a hug.

"Aw!" said Jig. "The girls have formed the Happy Support Society. We need a guys' version." He thumped Cameron's shoulder. "You're so good. Maybe not as fast or smart as your brother, but you can do this, buddy."

Cameron started to growl but turned it into a laugh to shut the guy up. Jig was as transparent as air. Maybe his deflation techniques worked on other people, but not on Cameron. He *wasn't* as fast as Spencer. But he might be as smart, even smarter. Either way, he was here.

The door opened again, this time to the tear-streaked face of Dacey. "Well, I'm going home, y'all. To nightmares about keys fallin' all over me." She came around and gave each one a two-armed hug.

Estella hugged back with only one.

Cameron wished he could have filmed that.

Bill came in with a large purse. "Is this what you asked for, Dacey?"

"Thanks, Bill."

"Just make it quick." Bill backed away.

Dacey pulled out a sheet of paper. "Could y'all sign this? On the front, if you don't mind. It's for my scrapbook, though I can't end the book like I'd planned." She handed it to Cameron along with a pink sparkle pen.

Was this what he thought it was? A sketch of the obstacle course? Could he get one?

Cameron signed his name and passed it on.

Jig took it. "What is this?"

"That stadium study guide I was talking about. If y'all brought yours, I'll sign 'em, too."

"I didn't get a picture," Jig said. "Anyone else get a picture?"

The others hadn't, either.

"Well, maybe you got something I didn't. But that's not important," said Dacey. "Please sign it, y'all, while I apologize to Estella."

"Me?"

Dacey nodded. "I was rude today. Truth is, you're

so pretty you kept remindin' me of Laura, and well, she just gets to me. Makes me ugly. And now I'm goin' out there to fake-smile at her, and we'll both pretend we're besties."

"You do that," said Estella. "It's been interesting meeting you."

"Likewise." Dacey tucked the sketch back into her purse, pageant-waved, and walked out the door.

Bill leaned in. "I'll be right back for your next little adventure."

"What was that about?" said Jig. "If I had a picture—"

"Does it matter?" said Estella. "You're still here, and she's not."

Apparently, it mattered to Jig. "Why'd she get a picture and I didn't?" he asked when Bill came back a couple of minutes later.

"These Games are full of surprises, aren't they?"

"But—"

"You want to play, Jig? Or you want to talk?"

"Bring it on!" said Jig.

Bill smiled. "Hold on to your seats. Here we go!"

The lounge veered backward, then toward the left,

before it came to a smooth stop. It opened to a waiting area painted like a busy foreign marketplace with stalls of fruits and rugs and jewelry, people in colorful clothes, dogs and kids running around.

"Same routine," said Bill. "Find your doors. Go in with the signal. And remember"—he paused for effect—"your door leads in, and your door leads out." He lifted his eyebrows a few times and smiled.

Ding! Ding! Ding!

Compared with the last room, this was like a closet, and it was totally bare except for a table and the objects on it: an empty tote bag, a pad of paper, pens, a bolted-down GollyReader, and his next challenge card.

When last we left Tad (young Thaddeus G. Golliwop), he was ordering lunch for old Uncle Eb. Today he's faced with another task. He must do the marketing for Eb's brother, old Uncle Zeb.

One problem: Young Tad is strapped for time and needs your help. Go to the market and bring back the four items Uncle Zeb needs, one each from the four appropriate stalls. Make sure you also pick up the corresponding price tags so you will know the appropriate prices.

When you return from your shopping trip, figure out how much Zeb owes, then post that exact amount to Zeb's account. (One-minute penalty for each wrong guess.)

And the four items? Uncle Zeb is hard to figure out, but this might help:

He'll buy organic deviled eggs, but not organic egg rolls.

He'll buy homemade fruitcake, but not store-bought cupcakes.

He loves crab cakes, but not shrimp rolls.

And palm nuts? Yes! But not pecans or walnuts or Brazil nuts or most other types of nuts.

Grocery shopping? Not high on Cameron's Hooray List, but this wasn't really shopping. This was cracking Uncle Zeb's code. Why did he like those foods? What common thread would show Cameron exactly what to buy?

At the top of Uncle Zeb's like list: organic deviled eggs. What made them organic? Organic chickens? Organic ingredients? What ingredients went into deviled eggs? No. This wasn't a cooking show.

New tactic. Why organic deviled eggs? Why not spicy deviled eggs or purple deviled eggs? Or organic scrambled eggs?

But no egg rolls. So the word "egg" wasn't the key. Neither was "organic." And homemade fruitcake? Weren't there like a million fruitcake jokes, how horrible they were? Wouldn't the whole world trade a fruitcake for a cupcake?

Crab cakes and shrimp rolls. So it had nothing to do with cakes and nothing to do with rolls and nothing to do with seafood allergies.

Allergies? Was Zeb allergic to nuts? And if you're allergic to nuts, do palm nuts count?

Cameron laughed. This wasn't a medical show, either. He needed to focus on the words and their letters.

What did the words in the yes column have in common?

Cameron wrote them in reverse order to see it differently:

Palm nuts
Crab cakes
Homemade fruitcake
Organic deviled eggs

Two words, two words, two words, three words. Some words started with vowels; others, consonants. No pattern to the second letters or the third letters or the letters they ended with. There were letters with ascenders and descenders and letters without. There were letters with curves and letters with straight lines and combinations of the two. And his brain was about to overheat again.

There had to be some pattern he wasn't seeing yet. It wouldn't be spelling again, would it? Only one way to know: one letter at a time.

He went slowly, listening to the sound of the letters. "O-R-G-A-N-I-C-D-E-V-I-L-E-D-E-G-G-S.

"H-O-M-E-M-A-D-E-F-R-U-I-T-C-A-K-E.

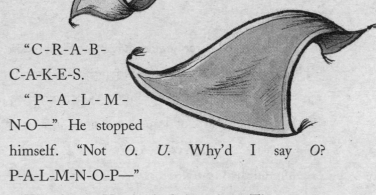

"C-R-A-B-C-A-K-E-S.

"P-A-L-M-N-O—" He stopped himself. "Not *O. U.* Why'd I say *O*? P-A-L-M-N-O-P—"

Was that it? He checked the others. The *a–b–c* in "crab cakes" and the *d–e–f* in "homemade fruitcake" and the *c–d–e* in "organic deviled eggs." On the don't buy side? None had three consecutive letters of the alphabet. Time to shop! But where? As Bill had said, his door led in and his door led out.

Cameron grabbed the tote bag and puzzle card and hoped the painted market in the common hall had magically transformed into a real one. No such luck, but one of four new doors there had his name.

Inside *was* a marketplace. Magic carpets soared in midair. Live parrots squawked from the corners. It even smelled like cinnamon and curry and other exotic spices. Most important, each stall, billowing with brilliant fabric, had a sign bearing its name.

Which four, out of all these

dozens, contained three sequential letters?

He surveyed the signs from where he was standing. FRANK'S FRANKS. No. JAKE SANTANGELO'S GREEN GROCERY. Lots of letters, but none in a row. SAM STUART'S SAUSAGES & SUCH. Yes!

Sam's stall had four choices:

Hot dogs
Polish sausage
Bratwurst
Salami

Cameron tossed the package of bratwurst into his tote.

He ruled out Ethel Toffel's Cakes 'n' Bakes, then moved around to another row of stalls. Not Fernando's Foods, but yes to Raj Klondike's Condiments. His choices:

Orange marmalade
Prickly pear jelly
Litchi jam
Persimmon puree

In went the litchi jam and—

He looked at the space where the jam used to be. A slip of paper. "Litchi jam: $1.00–$2.00."

He ran back to the sausage shop. The price slip was there. "Bratwurst: $4.00–$5.00."

Couldn't they be more specific? He'd figure that out later. He bypassed Paul's Poultry, Super Spicy Spices, and Candies by Candy. But he stopped at B.C. Dinners. His choices:

Chicken fricassee
Beef goulash
Turkey hash
Ham and beans

In went the beef goulash and the price tag. "Beef goulash: $3.00–$4.00."

Next stop, Lehi Juarez's Tex-Mex.

Poblano pepper poppers
Toasty tostadas
Hot tamales
Fresh frijoles

He popped in the poppers and their $2.00–$3.00 price, then sprinted back to his room.

He plopped the tote on the desk and dug out the price tags. How much should he add to Zeb's account? How much should he enter into the GollyReader? He laid out the price tags in order of cost. $1.00–$2.00. $2.00–$3.00. $3.00–$4.00. $4.00–$5.00. The cost was anywhere from $10 to $14. Did Uncle Zeb pay whatever he wanted? If only it were that easy. If only there weren't penalties involved.

Had the instructions said anything other than "appropriate prices"? No.

What would be appropriate for bratwurst? "Just tell me how much," he said into the air. He turned the slips over in case he'd missed something, but they were blank on the back.

A door slammed. Either someone had just left or someone had come out. Or maybe . . .

Was Jig heading for the trunks? Were the prices in the trunks? Should he look?

No. He wasn't desperate. Yet. Cameron took a deep breath. He needed to slow down, find the pattern. He'd already figured out the appropriate stalls and appropriate foods. And there was that word again. "Appropriate." Appropriate prices. So all the groceries had three letters in order and all the stall names had three letters in order. And . . .

That had to be it! Appropriate prices. Three numbers in order. He wrote those down:

$ 1.23
2.34
3.45
4.56
$11.58

Was that it? Was there any other way to look at it? His mind was a total blank. Fine.

He hit the one. One again. Decimal point. Five. Eight. He paused. He could lose a minute by sitting and staring or he could hit Enter and see if he was right. He hit Enter.

The screen went blank. The door opened behind him.

Cameron raised his hands in victory. But then the door closed.

CHAPTER 28

Cameron's face went cold. Had he lost? He tried the door. Still locked. Back to the desk. Hit the GollyReader. Dark.

The door clicked. Cameron turned. Bill.

"Is this is it?" Cameron asked. "Time to say good-bye?"

"Yep. Good-bye to the market. Good-bye to bratwurst. And hello to the lounge."

"Huh?"

"I could have fun tormenting you, but nah." Bill laughed. "There was someone else coming through, so we locked you back in until the coast was clear."

"I got it right?"

Bill slapped him on the back. "You're even first. Hope you don't mind being alone in the lounge. This might take a while."

Alone was fine. Alone was quiet. Alone, he could smell himself. He went into the bathroom. Its closet was stocked with stacks of towels and toothbrushes, hairbrushes and hair spray, deodorants and colognes. And it had a mirror.

He was a sweaty mess. Cameron turned the water on full force, doused his head, and practically drenched his whole Gollywhopper shirt. He took it off and tried to towel-dry it. While he was half undressed, he soaped up one of the smaller towels and rubbed down his arms and torso. He rinsed, dried, sprayed on deodorant, then put his slightly smelly shirt back on.

Maybe some cologne? He'd never worn any before. He sprayed some onto a towel and took a whiff. Whew! Um, no. He sprayed a different one. Better, but if he smelled like someone else, he might play like someone else. And he was doing pretty well with his own smells. Besides, he didn't need Jig calling him Cologne Boy.

He swished around a swig of mouthwash, ran his fingers through his hair like he did every morning, and spit. Then he got out another small towel, cleaned the splattered water—his mom would be proud—and headed back out.

Still deserted. But then a chair swiveled toward him. Clio. "And I thought girls took forever in the bathroom."

Cameron looked around. "There are two. You could have—"

She laughed. "Just kidding, Cameron. I've been here only a minute. But you look better."

How'd he look before?

She laughed some more. "You don't say much, but your face says everything. You didn't look horrible before. Just a little wild."

"You look the same. How do you stay so calm?"

"Calm?" She took in a breath. "If you X-rayed my insides, you'd see a party of swords and bullets and tornados. But if I sit here and breathe and drum on my leg and watch something mindless and distracting, the tornados might downgrade from EF-fives to EF-twos."

So she wasn't perfect.

"Do you need to talk," said Clio, "or are you okay if I put on my headphones?"

"I'm good."

"You are." She smiled like she meant it and turned away.

Cameron tried a mindless TV rerun himself. The episode finished, and soon after the next one started, in came Estella.

She looked around, eyes wide, neck craning like she didn't know if she was first or last.

Time to put her out of her misery. Cameron stood.

"Who else?" she said, her eyes still big.

Cameron spun Jig's empty chair around.

Her eyes got even bigger. "He's not here? I beat him?" She danced Cameron around.

He was so glad for the deodorant.

Clio came out of her cocoon and joined in their celebration.

The door banged open. Bill pushed Jig through, then held him at arm's length with one hand and slammed the door behind them with the other. "And now the cameras can't see you, Jig. So, calmly. What do you want to know?"

"The trunks weren't in our conference room. How was I supposed to know where they were? And when I finally found them, what'd they have? Money and games. Where were the real price tags? Not that price range junk. Not—"

It was like Jig finally realized Clio and Cameron were there. "What are you looking at? This little party of yours won't last. They're gonna figure out they forgot to give me the prices."

Bill put a hand on his shoulder, but Jig threw it off.

Clio walked up to him. "Jig."

He stared past her.

"You've been so cool," she said. "You really want to go out like this? You want the world to see you ranting like a maniac?"

His neck twitched.

"We didn't need the trunks, Jig," she said. "We had to figure out that the prices went one, two, three like the words went a, b, c."

He dropped into Clio's chair and put his head in his hands. "I psyched myself out," he said. "*You* were supposed to hunt for the trunks. *I* was supposed to figure it out. I needed a break. I was only going to look for a minute." He shook his head. "How did someone like me believe my own mess of manure?" He kept muttering, and they all backed away.

Bill gave him a couple of minutes, then came up to him. "Ready to face the cameras?"

Jig signaled he needed another minute, rocked his head back and forth, circled it a few times, planted a smile, and stood. "It's been real." He rushed out the door.

Bill followed but came right back in. "How much time do you need, Estella? We can't give you a lot, but would fifteen minutes do it?"

"I can go right now," she said, "but five minutes would be great."

"You got it."

She headed to the bathrooms and came out a few minutes later. "If that had a shower, I'd move in. Did you see the closet? It has everything." She smelled her wrist. "Mmm. I've gotta get me some of this."

"Some of what?" Bill said, popping his head back in the door.

"The perfume. The one with the spiraly top."

Bill walked into the bathroom, then came out holding a bottle. "This one?"

Estella nodded.

"Yours!" He put it on a table. "It'll be here when you're all done. But now, time to see what's next."

"You already know what it is, Bill," said Estella. "Give us a clue?"

"Sit," he said, "and I'll give you the entire challenge."

They stared at him, waiting. The room moved, but he stayed silent.

"You really thought—" The room stopped. "I meant I'd *take* you to the challenge." Bill opened the door to a hall with plain walls. "Things are a little different this time," he said, positioning them at their doors. "And that's all, except good luck! You may need it."

Three eerie musical notes sounded. Cameron's door opened to a small room with a chair, clothes and gear, a set of double doors, and the challenge card on a table.

* * * *

DIAMOND VALLEY DEMONS
(New from GollyVideo)

The Demons have stolen all the diamonds, the lifeblood of Diamond Valley. Without the magical gems, crops are failing, structures are disintegrating, floods follow droughts, stones turn to dust, and the good people of Diamond Valley are fading fast. Because you discovered one of the last remaining DiamondSabres, it's your charge to reclaim five pounds of diamonds and restore life to this vital city.

Before you battle:

1. GEAR UP. Don the DemonFighter suit, shoes, and goggles. Only then may you enter.

2. CARRY THEM. Your GatherBag and DiamondSabre are the only two battle items you may bring into your mission.

3. WEIGH THEM. Your scale is in the Battle Antechamber. WARNING: Before you enter, you must fully remove every bit of battle gear. If the scale shows you have not collected

enough diamonds, reenter Diamond Valley, gear up again, and finish your task. Bring all the diamonds you've collected with you. (They are not safe in the Battle Antechamber.)

Follow all directions or stiff penalties will apply. Good luck!

Cameron's muscles revved for action. He grabbed the suit from its hook and the boots from the floor. He pulled off his shoes, stepped into the one-piece DemonFighter suit, and fastened the Velcro tabs.

The boots were exactly his size. How'd they know? Didn't matter. He adjusted the goggles over his eyes and felt like a giant fly. How weird did he look? Didn't matter, either. He hung the cross-body GatherBag over his right shoulder so it hung on his left hip.

Now for the DiamondSabre. It had some heft to it, but it wasn't unwieldy. He could reach two of its three buttons with the fingers of his right hand, but he'd need to use his left to press the third. None of them worked. Maybe they'd activate once he got inside. He took one last look at the instructions. He was geared up. He had his two battle items. Time to get the diamonds.

He pushed through the double doors, but he hadn't expected this. The room was enormous. The skies were ominous. The landscape was ugly and parched, a real wasteland. A red cloud flew at him; it seemed so real he felt he could touch it and breathe it. These had to be 3-D goggles. And that had to be a Demon.

In came another Demon cloud and another. He lifted his sword to slice through the next one, but it turned and flew off. Wimp.

Time to see what these buttons did. The first let out a vibrating electrical bolt. The second—the Illuminator button—produced a light. He pointed it toward a boulder, and it illuminated a diamond-shaped mark. Diamonds underneath? He ran to lift the boulder, but a Demon charged. He raised the sword, but the Demon kept coming. He hit the first button and sent a jolt of electricity through the red cloud. It vaporized, but four more took its place.

He sent out another jolt. Pow! Another. Pow! Pow! Pow! He could advance again, but a giant green Demon swooped in and perched on the boulder.

Cameron pushed the button. The Green Demon laughed. Cameron tried to slice through it with his DiamondSabre. The sword bounced off the creature.

The third button! It sent out blue chomping light rays that surrounded the Green Demon and ate it to bits. A window in the Sabre's handle flashed a message: "You have two Light Brigades remaining."

He needed to be careful with those. He lifted the boulder and grabbed for the small pile of diamonds underneath, but more red clouds got in his face. He jolted eight away; then the Light Brigade button flashed once. Had he earned more? Next time he met a Green Demon, he'd find out.

He collected the diamonds under the rock and looked up. The ominous sky wasn't as dark. A few flowers had sprouted in the distance. "More diamonds!" he called. "Bring on the Demons!"

Two flew in his face. Pow! Pow! They scattered, and he pointed the Illuminator at a tree stump. The diamond symbol! Another Green Demon flew to guard it. What if he still had only two Light Brigades left? By the weight of his GatherBag, it would take more than three little mounds of diamonds to win this challenge.

Maybe there was another way to lure the Green Demon off the stump. He charged it. Poked it. Prodded it. Speared it. Screamed at it. Illuminated it. He was about to spit at it, but that wouldn't work. It was immune to everything except the Light Brigade. He hit the third button. The Light Brigade vaporized it. The Sabre flashed the same message: "You have two Light Brigades remaining."

"All right!" He *had* gained a Light Brigade by slaying the Red Demons.

How many would it take, though? He slew three more. The button didn't flash. Two more. Nothing. Another five. Flash! Pow! Pow! Pow! He fought off ten more. Flash! He had earned two more Light Brigades!

He ran at a Green Demon laughing at him from a garbage heap. "Laugh all you want, buddy. In a few seconds you won't have a mouth." He charged at it with the Light Brigade. Gone! "You have three Light Brigades remaining," flashed the message on his sword.

Yes! Cameron scooped up the diamonds. Fought more red guys. Gathered diamonds from the flower patch, from the wheelbarrow, from the bird's nest. The sky was now a light gray. How bright did it need to get before he had collected five pounds?

What did five pounds feel like? Somewhere between a baseball and a bowling ball, but that was no help. The bag didn't feel heavy enough anyway, and the sky was still gray. He flashed the Illuminator. There, in the cave! Got 'em! There, in the pond! That Green Demon wouldn't leave. He was out of Light Brigades.

"I need you, Red Demons!" He chased them over the hill and around the barn, loading his DiamondSabre with three Light Brigades and illuminating more diamonds along the way. Zap! He got the ones from the gopher hole. Zap! From the footbridge. Zap! From the pond.

The GatherBag was hanging much lower on his thigh. Five pounds yet? The clouds had given way to patches of blue and peeks of sun. The barn was in better repair, too. The barn had diamonds! Cameron jolted a whole army of Red Demons on his way. He added the barn stash to his bag.

Enough? If he took off his gear to weigh the

diamonds and was a single ounce short, he'd have to get dressed again. But it would also take time to fight Red Demons if he didn't have a Light Brigade left. New plan. He'd try for the diamonds in the shack, but if he was out of Light Brigades, he was done.

Third button. "Pow!"

The last Light Brigade left the DiamondSabre.

Cameron collected the stash. Now! Time to weigh! But where was the Battle Antechamber? He raced around the perimeter of Diamond Valley but didn't see a door. Maybe the Illuminator would.

He ran the length of one wall, shooting the Illuminator every couple of feet. Nothing. He turned the corner, and yes! Before he pushed the newly illuminated exit door, he lifted off the GatherBag, threw off his goggles, shoved off his boots, then wriggled out of his suit, leaving everything in a heap. His mother might have a fit, but he wouldn't score points for neatness.

He grabbed the diamonds, went out the door, and skidded in his socks to a stop in a hallway. This wasn't the Battle Antechamber. Where was it?

CHAPTER 29

Cameron turned right and ran along the curved hall. It kept curving. It was circular! He'd find his way eventually. Just wall. More wall. Then a door marked "Estella. Clio. Cameron!"

Inside, bathed in light, was the scale. He plunked the GatherBag on it. It did nothing. Oh! The bag. He dumped out the diamonds. A window lit: "6.14 lbs."

The door clicked open, and there was Bill, silent, holding another bag.

"So?" Cameron said.

"So what?"

"Am I in or out?"

"You're out," said Bill. "Out of Diamond Valley."

Cameron gave Bill a little push. "Stop scaring me like that."

"Then stop setting me up." Bill handed Cameron the bag. "You'll need these."

His shoes.

"Go put them on in the lounge. Meanwhile, I need to rescue Estella from Diamond Valley. Or maybe Diamond Valley needs to be rescued from Estella."

Clio turned from the refrigerator when he walked in. She held up a bowl of grapes. "Congrats! Want some?"

"Thanks." He broke off a bunch. "How long have you been here?"

"About ten minutes. Wasn't that great? The effects? The sun? Those Light Brigades? Loved it."

"You did?"

"Yes. I'm a girl, and I really did."

"Sorry," said Cameron. He popped some grapes into his mouth.

"It's okay. You couldn't know how much I love video games, the more swords the better. But you know what Diamond Demons needed? A whole waistband of weapons. Go in there with Diamond-Sabres blazing."

Cameron laughed. He'd be going head-to-head with Clio, with the best. It would have been more fun to beat Jig or Dacey. Wait. He'd already done that. He laughed some more, then turned it off when the door opened.

Estella shrugged. "I got carried away," she said. "Kept swinging at those Demons like there was no tomorrow. Except the green guys. They kept laughing at me until I learned how to vaporize them. Vaporized eight of them."

"How'd you do that?" Clio said. "Mine only had three blasts."

"Every time you slew ten of the red clouds, it reloaded another Light Brigade," said Estella. "How'd you do it without blasting them?"

"I dropped a few diamonds in another place; then one of the Green Demons left his post to come guard them. So I dropped four and collected a bigger pile. Repeat, repeat, repeat."

"And you got here faster than me," said Cameron.

"Faster than me, too." Estella sank into her chair. "The quiet here is so good. Getting out my frustrations, good. Facing Stephen again, very good. Winning some money, whatever money is in that trunk, excellent."

Bill came in.

"This is my cue to leave." Estella stood and gave Cameron a hug. "If it's not me, I'm glad it's you and Clio." She gave Clio an even bigger hug. "Thank you, friend." She let go and hugged her again. Then she broke free and headed to the door.

Bill held it open, then came right back in. "Five minutes or are you ready now?"

Cameron nodded at Clio.

"We're ready," she said.

"All right," said Bill. "One last time, hold on to your chairs."

The room moved.

"No Demons," said Bill. "No market. No barrage of keys." The room stopped. They stood, and Bill put an arm around each of them. "I would say, 'May the best contestant win,' but there is no better contestant here. I wish there were two prizes."

He positioned them inside a moonlit hall, and with the first few notes of "Twinkle, Twinkle Little Star," their doors opened.

Spanning the far wall of the vast and darkened

room were shelves crammed with boxes and boxes and boxes. It might not have been the entire Golly catalog, but there were enough toys and games to stock a whole toy store.

On a near table, next to a square object with a trigger handle, was the challenge card:

The day's been long, but you've been strong.
No need to tease, the rules are these:

1. You will be presented with a number of riddles.

2. The answer to each riddle is an object very closely associated with one or more of the Golly products before you.

3. When you figure out an answer, find an associated product.

4. Scan its UPC code with the scan gun provided.

5. For each correct scan, a puzzle piece will light up.

6. If you scan incorrectly, it will take two correct scans to light up your next piece.

7. The answer to some riddles will be associated with more than one product. You may scan up to two products for each answer, thus lighting up to two pieces per riddle.

8. When you can identify the puzzle picture, find the one associated product, grab it off the shelf, open it, and you will know what to do next.

"I hope I'll know," Cameron said to whoever was listening. But first, he needed riddles. No drawers in the table. Nothing else in the room, the ginormous room with the gigantic shelves and all those toys on all those shelves with all those colorful tabs sticking out. What were they?

Bookmark-sized riddles! Cameron gathered six of them. He read one. Then another. Then another. He shook his head. Why had he thought this would be quick or easy? He took the tabs back to the table and reread the blue one.

When you're down, you want to go up,
When you're up, you want to come down.
Here's one more clue: It's mixed up in delis,

No matter your city or town.

(Two puzzle pieces available.)

Up and down again. But why delis? Cameron started craving corned beef. Later.

So what goes up and down? An elevator? Yes, but he had to think toys. A sled. When you're at the bottom of the hill, you need to go up to ride down again. Same with the zip line. But where did the delis come in? Not just any delis, mixed-up ones.

No. "It's mixed up in delis." What did they mix up there? Batches of potato salad and coleslaw? People's orders; make sandwiches with the wrong meat? He needed to stop picturing plates of food. Why delis? Why not fast-food places or diners? Cameron had nothing.

He moved toward the Golly product wall for inspiration. The toys and games were stacked and packed solid. It almost made him dizzy. He drifted to the shelves of oversize items. Each seemed to have its own space, so it wasn't as overwhelming. They ran the gamut, from Aim Right Archery to Up 'n' Down Swing Set.

Up 'n' Down? Was that it? Cameron looked at the box.

"Includes swings, slide, gliding horse." Wait. Back up. The slide! Delis! Mixed up, the letters in "slide" spelled "delis"!

He grabbed the scanner from the table and pointed it at the UPC code. The scanner's display lit up: "Up 'n' Down Swing Set? If yes, scan again." He did. The scan gun went dark. But a little light came from above. One of the ceiling tiles now had pinpoints of color.

He needed to collect his second puzzle piece

available from that riddle. What else? A slide in a computer presentation? Golly didn't make those. Slide. Slide! In science! Microscope!

Cameron went to the *S*'s. Science the Golly Way! He scanned it twice. Another ceiling section lit with bits of color. No telling what the big picture was yet, but he knew what to do.

Next riddle. A green one.

I come all dressed in black and white.
My pedals pump a tad.
Just touch the keys and you will please
Unless your playing's sad.
(One puzzle piece available.)
✳ ✳ ✳ ✳

Key? Pedals? Black and white? His dad watched an old TV show where they called police cars "black-and-whites." And cars have keys. And pedals that don't move much. At least they don't appear to. Timothy's parents let him back the car out of the driveway, but Cameron's didn't. If he won, he'd take himself to the go-cart track. He'd been sick last month for Sameer's birthday party there.

It was getting harder and harder to focus. He needed to push through. Black and white. Okay. Pedals. Fine. But touching keys? Just touching a car key wouldn't start the car; you have to actually *turn* it. And you don't exactly think of cars as pleasing. Black and white with keys and a pedal and something you played.

Was it this easy? Piano? Maybe so. This riddle scored only one puzzle piece. Maybe the two-piecers were harder.

He ran to the *P* section. No piano. But Golly made one. What did they call it? Baby Grand by Golly! Over to the *B*'s.

He scanned the box twice. Looked up. Another piece, more pinpricks of light, but unconnected to the others. It looked familiar but not enough to risk a guess.

Next. He picked up another blue riddle, but it was the same as the first blue. The second green was a repeat, too. He tried orange.

Head, sweat, or waist,
you may find at my left hand.
And at my right hand,
you may find leader, width, or stand.
(Two puzzle pieces available.)

Where should he start here? With the repeated word: "hand." A person has hands. A clock has hands. Animals have paws. Except gorillas and chimps? Were theirs called hands and feet? Even they don't have heads near any hands. Waists, either. You could have sweaty hands, but unless you're some muscle-bound freak, you can't exactly hold a leader, like a president, in one hand.

It didn't say anything about holding. Head, sweat, or waist might be at the left hand; leader, width, or stand, at the right. Did all of them need to be there at the same time? If they did, it would say "and" instead of "or." So sometimes he'd find one of the things—

Things? Not necessarily. What if they were talking about words? Words on the left hand that came before some other word. Words on the right that came after.

Worth a try. First, "head." Head what? Head case? If they made him think much more, he'd turn into a real head case. Head what? Headlines? Headquarters? Headphones? No, no, and no. Head. Head. Headache. This was giving him a headache. Forget "head."

"Sweat"? He wasn't going there, not the way his own head was sweating. And "waist"? He could only think of the other waist: waste can, wasteland, waste away.

He switched to the words on the right: "leader, width, or stand." Something leader. Something leader. Fearless leader? World leader? World! At least a good word. But it would be worldwide, not world width.

Cameron started to shake his head, but his neck was stiff. His whole body felt encased in cement. Should he switch riddles? Not yet. He'd already invested this much time. He sat on the desk, closed his eyes, and took a couple of deep breaths. He needed to slow down. One word: "stand." Headstand? No. "Head" was on the list already. Handstand? They wouldn't give the answer in the clue. But his brain kept repeating it. Handstand. Handstand. Hand width. Hand leader. Head hand. Sweat hand. Yeah, sweaty hands.

He felt like something was there. Something was just off. Waist hand. Hand leader. Hand leader. He closed his eyes and listened to his mind saying that again. Hand leader. Hand leader. And then came his trumpet. And then Mr. Wichter, the band teacher. Bandleader! Bandwidth! Bandstand! Waistband, sweatband, headband!

He was in business! Two puzzle pieces. He ran straight to the One-Man-Band Show, a favorite when he was little. He scanned it twice but didn't take time to see the new puzzle piece. He ran to the B's, to the classic Golly game Band of Thieves. He scanned it. Scanned it again. Now he looked up.

Four of the pieces were connected. Four brightly colored pieces with . . .

Fireworks! He'd read about Golly's game called The Fireworks Factory, but he'd never seen it. If he'd never seen it, why did the picture up there look so familiar? Where had—

Cameron felt like he was going to throw up. He'd seen it before, that exact picture. Today. The TV control center. All those monitors. Blank except for three with fireworks. No wonder he ID'd the puzzle picture so fast: He'd seen it before!

He ran to the shelf. Pulled out The Fireworks Factory. All he had to do was open it, the instructions said. Open it and he'd know what to do.

Only he didn't know what to do. He could open it and win. No one would know he'd seen the picture on those screens. It wasn't his fault someone had left the door open. It wasn't his fault.

Happenings like this, so random and unpredictable, were part of the game, part of any game, right? If an umpire missed seeing a tag in baseball, the runner was still safe. If a piece of debris knocked out an Indy car, the other cars went on. If Cameron had been a golf ball expert, he wouldn't have disqualified himself from that question about dimples.

No one would have expected him to.

He needed to open that box. This was his time. To know how it felt to be Spencer. To be celebrated, be on top. His best chance, his one chance to win. He would be the new champion of the Gollywhopper Games, and no one could take that away from him. No one would know how he'd won.

Except he would know. Cameron would know.

"Bill!" he called at the top of his lungs. "Bill! I have a problem. A big one!"

CHAPTER 30

Bill rushed in. "You okay? Bleeding? Dying?" He looked at The Fireworks Factory on the table, glanced toward the ceiling.

"I don't know what to do," said Cameron.

Bill shook his head. "The instructions are clear."

"It's not the instructions. If I open this, I'll win. I know it."

"Then what's the problem?"

"I don't want to be a cheater," Cameron said. "This morning I came out of the bathroom and thought Sharryn might be in an open office down the hall. She wasn't, but the TV monitors were showing these fireworks." Cameron pointed to the ceiling. "Which is why I recognized the picture so fast. So I don't know what to do."

Bill put a hand against the headphone on his right ear. Nodded. Looked up.

"What'd they say? I'm a loser?"

"Oh, no," said Bill. "You're not a loser, Cameron." He clamped him on the back. "You're the best. It took guts to do what you just did." With a hand still on Cameron's back, Bill guided him back to the lounge. "Clio's on her way. And once she gets here—"

The door opened. "She's here."

She rushed over to Cameron. "What's wrong? They said you had a problem."

"I'm okay," he said.

"Then what?"

"There was a glitch," said Bill. "Cameron unintentionally saw something that gave him an unfair advantage. So we'll be giving you an alternate challenge. A do-over."

Clio looked at Cameron. "You would have won?"

"We'll never know, Clio," said Bill, "and we won't start speculating. Right now we need you both to sit and put on your headphones. We'll pump in two minutes of music to give you a breather, then we'll start again like nothing happened."

Bill turned their chairs away from each other.

Like nothing happened? Something *had* happened. He might have won. He could have been a millionaire. If this had been him against Jig or Dacey, maybe he would have pretended nothing happened.

Cameron pounded his fist once into his chair. He'd been cruising with that puzzle. Who knew if he could solve the next one? He was probably, once again, on his way to becoming Cameron, the runner-up in a two-person contest. At least he was used to that. He couldn't get used to being a cheater.

If only he'd stayed by the bathroom. If only he hadn't looked into that room. If only he'd asked Sharryn about the fireworks on the monitor. If only . . .

The room started moving. He needed to regroup. He still had a chance, but that chance was against a competitor maybe as strong as Spencer.

The room stopped. They stepped out.

"Good luck, Clio."

She gave him a hug. "Good luck yourself."

They parted. Cameron's door was on the left; Clio's, on the right.

The buzzer sounded. Beyond the door was the puzzle/stunt area, either theirs or the Orange Team's. Cameron couldn't tell. He picked up the card on a long table at the entrance.

This room should look familiar,
exactly as before.
You worked the puzzles and the stunts,
and now you're back for more.
The games and toys unused back then?
They're waiting here for you.
Collect your unused choices;
then we'll tell you what to do.

No map? Spencer had once joked that Cameron could get lost going from his bedroom to the kitchen. He breathed in. He breathed out. He'd tried. He'd tried to remember where everything was.

He couldn't panic, though. Clio might beat him navigating the area, but they'd need to do something with the toys and games after, wouldn't they? He could make up time unless he stood here like a Popsicle.

What were the choices from their last puzzle? The numbered doors. They were close, near the Rainbow Maze, but they now had a sign. YOU WILL NOT NEED THESE DOORS. COLLECT ONLY THE TOYS AND GAMES IN THEIR BOXES.

Perfect. He didn't need the only one he could find fast. Now where? All he saw were the refrigerator, the sailboat, the blinking bank of lights. He needed to go wide angle. He looked far and up. The ceiling! The cow jumping over the moon. The greased pigs! He ran, focusing on the cow, and bumped into the broccoli, barely missed the car,  and scooted around the scuba divers. There they were, still on a blue-lit table. He grabbed LionPaws and DoomTomb.

But those had led to the second stunt, the one with

the mice. So where were . . .

He ran to the blue door where they'd originally entered. Blue-lit table! Jupiter Fighter and Agree to Disagree.

Nothing on the boxes told him what to do. Maybe something would magically happen when he collected them all. He still needed four more. He could run faster empty-handed, and he wasn't that far from the puzzle table. He dropped the boxes there.

Now where? What was left? The mouse cage and the nose. The nose, the nose . . .

Oh, yeah! In one of the far corners, but to the right? To the left? His feet veered to the right. Please, please, please . . .

Yes! The table! Things that Go Bump and Baby Chat-a-Lot.

Now to the mouse cage! Which was . . .

Cameron looked up. He saw the snowcapped mountain, the huge lightbulb, the Leaning Tower of Pisa, but he had no memory of where JinxTrap was. If he could find the dressers or the giant school supplies, he'd be there. But where was *there*?

He did the only thing he could do. He ran. He ran all the way to the front of the room but didn't find the mouse cage. He moved about six feet over and snaked his way to the back. No trap, no dressers, no supplies.

He moved over again. To the front. To the back. Nowhere. He stopped five seconds to breathe, he hoped not five seconds too long. Then again, if he passed out, that would take longer than five seconds.

He sprinted back toward the front. And there it was! The tip of a giant pencil! He circled the school supplies. The table! He snatched up Supreme Dazzlers and RetroWars.

Now where was the challenge table? Near the front. Which was front? He looked around again. Toward the ceiling. The cow and moon were toward the back. He ran the opposite way. The long table! And now it had words projected on its surface: "Open the only choice that has more vowels than consonants in its name."

"Okay." He breathed. "Good." Breathed. "Easy."

Cameron spread the eight boxes across the table.

Supreme Dazzlers

RetroWars

Agree to Disagree

LionPaws

Baby Chat-a-Lot

Things that Go Bump

DoomTomb

Jupiter Fighters

Sweat dripped on DoomTomb. He hoped it wasn't an omen. And he knew it wasn't the right choice. Which one was, though?

It had to be Agree to Disagree. One, two, three, four, five, six, seven, eight vowels. Five, seven, eight, nine, ten . . . fifteen letters total. More vowels than consonants.

Inside the box was a switch. No instructions, but it was obvious. He flipped it.

The whole back wall of the warehouse went dark, then relit with Agree to Disagree. The words flashed once before all the letters fizzled. Wait. Not all. Two of them came back up in a laserlike zigzag of lights. The *A* and the *T*. They each pulsed off, then on with a different musical note.

He sensed a glow behind him. There were words projected on the large front wall: "Open the choice that has no repeating letters."

No-brainer. He opened LionPaws. Flipped the switch. The front wall went dark. LionPaws came up. All those letters fizzled out except the *O* and *N*. They also pulsed with musical notes.

The next clue lit the right wall. "Open the choice that has the most words in its name."

Hooray for easy! Things that Go Bump. Switch, flipped. Right wall, dark. Words: "Things that Go Bump." Fizzle. The *N* and *M* stayed with two more musical notes.

All those letters had to be spelling something. Just one more wall left. "Open the remaining box, whose middle three letters can spell a type of tree."

Five left: Supreme Dazzlers, RetroWars, Baby Chat-a-Lot, DoomTomb, and Jupiter Fighters. He didn't see a tree right away. He needed pencil and paper. He wrote: SUPREME DAZZLERS. Fifteen letters. He crossed off the first six letters and the last six letters and left *E D A* in the middle. No matter how he mixed those up, no tree. Next.

RETROWARS. Nine letters. He circled the three in the middle. *R O W*? Row? A word, but not a tree he knew. Next!

BABYCHATALOT. Twelve letters. No way to have three letters in the middle unless they meant three of the middle letters. Take four off one side and four off the other, and he was left with *C H A T*. Choose three. Cat tree? No. Hat tree? Was that a real thing? Maybe. Act tree. Tac tree. Too many maybes. He hoped there'd be a more definite answer. Next.

DOOMTOMB. *O M T O* in the middle. Mot? Tom ? Moo? Too? Nope. And choosing three of four letters in the middle wasn't the way Golly operated. One more.

JUPITERFIGHTERS. Fifteen letters again. He eliminated the first six and last six. Three in the middle: *R F I*. Rif? No. Fir. Fir tree! He opened that box. Flipped the switch. "Jupiter Fighters" lit on the left wall. All the letters fizzled except *U* and *I*.

Everything went dark for a moment; then, one at a time, the letters flashed briefly, randomly on the walls to his front, back, left, and right. He tried to follow them, but all that turning and flashing made him dizzy. He wrote down the eight letters. *T A O N N M U I*

If he rearranged them correctly, he'd know what to do. He stopped, took a breath. And what was that sound? He'd totally forgotten the musical notes, a simple scale, do-re-me-fa-so-la-ti, one note for each letter. He heard the first note, *do*, from the wall on his right. He turned, but too late to see the corresponding letter. *Re* sounded from the front wall. *Me* from the left wall, and he caught it. The note came with the letter *U*. If *me* was the third note in the scale, *U* was the third letter!

He waited for the scale to start again. It would start from the wall on the right. After that he'd get ready to look front.

Wait for it. Wait for it. Go!

Do was the letter *M. Re* was *O*. Then the *U* he already had. He caught the *fa* on the front wall. *N!*

M O U N . . .

It had to be the mountain in the middle of the warehouse. No time to check. He raced to the mountain. Hoped he'd know what to do. Hoped he was fast enough. Hoped he—

Bzzzz!

Rumbling. Popping. His letters stopped flashing. The notes stopped playing. Fireworks, projected on the ceiling. And a picture of Clio up there. And he knew.

CHAPTER 31

Bill and Carol each had a hand on Cameron's back. He couldn't bear to meet their eyes, see the "Sorry" looks on their faces. He hung his head.

"Buddy. Look at me," said Bill. "Remember after the team competition when I said I couldn't be prouder? I lied. I am even more proud now. And I doubt I will ever be prouder of anyone than I am of you."

Cameron dug his fingers into his leg, trying to stop the tears.

"Cameras are off," Carol said. "Cry, scream, anything."

A few tears came. A few more. He looped his thumb under the neck of his shirt and wiped his eyes. He leaned onto a giant stack of foam pancakes and put his head, facedown, on his arms like his first-grade teacher had always made them do when the class had gotten too noisy, though he had never been the one making noise.

And now he'd always wonder why he'd picked that moment, the moment he recognized the fireworks, to speak loudly for the first time in his life. He should have won when he'd had the chance. Funny, though, he wasn't truly sorry. He wouldn't have been able to celebrate. Not really.

He lifted his head and looked at their faces. "I'm okay. I am. Now what?"

"Short interview," said Bill, "but only when you're ready."

"I'm ready."

"Our announcer, Randy Wright, will ask you some questions," said Bill. "What was the competition like? What's Clio like? And he will ask you about the fireworks puzzle. Why did you admit you'd seen the answer? Did you remember there was a million dollars on the line?"

Cameron let out a sad laugh. "I remembered."

"I know," said Bill. "And that's why we're all so, so proud here."

"Proud enough to give me a million dollars anyway?"

Bill opened his mouth. Closed it.

Cameron laughed for real. "Just kidding."

"Good," said Bill, "because I don't think two million dollars is in our budget."

Bill and Carol took him to a room with dark-draped walls on three sides and a camera and two stools near the green screen on the fourth. Randy Wright came up and shook Cameron's hand. "This will be painless, I promise. We just want the honest truth. If you need a break, pause after your answer and let me know."

Randy Wright asked exactly what Bill had said.

Yes, Cameron was disappointed, but he'd tried as hard as he could. Yes, it had been hard work, and if anyone knew how to stop his head from sweating, he'd appreciate it. From off camera, Bill threw a towel in his face. He laughed and wiped his head.

There would be life after losing. He'd go home and make a video out of this and post it online. And maybe he could get a hundred people to watch it.

Immediately After
THE GAMES

Bert Golliwop wondered if he looked as pale as he felt. Was it fury? Was it relief? Was he coming down with that mysterious flu?

Tawkler from Marketing led the rest of the team into Bert's office. "The kid saved us," she said. "We need to capitalize somehow. Give him a huge bonus. The publicity will more than pay for it."

"Not so fast," said Morrison from Legal. "We also have to deal with the other issue, the one surrounding the Dahlgren girl and that obstacle course picture. While the contract does hold us harmless should circumstances beyond our control give one contestant advantage over another, we need to be cautious."

"No one needs to know about Dacey," said Plago. "It was in the privacy of the lounge."

"We know about it," said Morrison. "The other contestants know about it, and that means the world will know about it. What else have we learned?"

Bert nodded at Tawkler, who said, "Mr. Golliwop, Danny, and I just finished speaking with Dacey. She received the obstacle course picture as she was on her way out of the arena. When we asked who had given it to her, she pointed toward Danny and said it was a cute guy who looked something like him."

"Aha!" said Jenkins. "It's been Danny all along."

"Oh, no," said Bert Golliwop. "He was with Gil in New England, and she was in an arena in Georgia."

"Kids like him have friends," Jenkins said. "Maybe they're in cahoots."

"Speculation proves nothing," said Morrison. "We need facts. And we need to worry. As I said, there are rules. The FCC will scrutinize."

"Maybe a little scrutiny would be good," said Tawkler. "Maybe they'll find our traitor."

"No," said Bert. "We'll find our traitor. I've already hired the best security team in the country."

"But the Games are over," said Larraine from Finance. "There's no profit in hiring a security team."

Jenkins backed away from her. "It's you!"

"What?" she said.

"You don't want investigators because you're the mole."

"I am not. I just don't see any financial upside. If you want to hire them, go for it."

"I am going for it," said Bert, "because no one sticks a mole in my company and gets away with it. Besides, what other company secrets might this mole take back to Flummox? And what if we want to do the Gollywhopper Games again next year?"

Tawkler rubbed her hands together. "You'd do this again next year?"

"Absolutely," said Bert. "But not until we find that mole."

CHAPTER 32

After the interview Bill brought Cameron back to the lounge.

"Cameron!" Clio ran up and hugged him. "What happened? Can we talk about it, Bill?"

"You can talk about anything," he said. "And congratulations, by the way. Why aren't you screaming and jumping?"

"I'm still in shock. I know for a fact that screaming and jumping will happen, but right now I'm really confused."

Cameron told her about the fireworks. "It didn't even register until the fifth piece lit up."

"Fifth piece? Seriously? I only had two. It took me

forever to find the riddles. I even turned the table and chair over before I got smart." She looked Cameron straight in the eye. "Picture or no picture, you would have won." She turned to Bill. "He would have won. He deserves to win."

"We don't know that," said Bill.

"Then he deserves half my money," she said.

"We can't do that," Bill said. "Part of what you signed and what your parents signed prohibits two contestants from splitting the cash. You'd win nothing. Neither would he. We can't have two of you working together to the exclusion of others. Today you won the whole thing or nothing."

Cameron nodded. "Maybe they shouldn't have left the picture on the screens, but I wasn't supposed to be there. Anyway, I won something." He looked at Bill. "There is money in my trunk, right?"

"You want to see for yourself later," said Bill, "or do you want me to tell you now?"

"Tell me."

"It started at ten thousand dollars, but each time a person was eliminated, we fattened it by five thousand a pop. So there's twenty-five."

"Thousand?"

"Yes, thousand."

Cameron grinned. "Not a million, but what kid wins twenty-five thousand dollars? I'm good."

"I know you are," Bill said.

The door opened, and the moms, the dads, Clio's sister, and Cameron's brothers, and Janae rushed them like a swarm of locusts.

Clio finally started jumping and screaming and acting like someone who'd won a million dollars.

Cameron shook his head.

"I know," said his mom.

His dad had Cameron's shoulder in a wonderful vise grip.

It was just the three of them. The interviewer had pulled Spencer and Walker aside to ask them some questions.

"You'll earn your million dollars another way. I have no doubt," said his dad.

His mom nodded. "You'll be the one who can afford to support us in our old age." She gave her that's-a-joke laugh. "We tell that to everyone."

"You don't tell me."

"We thought you knew," his dad said.

Cameron shook his head. "You're always saying stuff like that to Spencer. And making sure Walker is brushing his teeth. But I'm just sort of . . . there."

"Oh, Cameron." His mom gave him a hug. "Walker's still young. And Spencer needs those words. Always has. But you. It's like you were born to have a real chance, more than anyone I know . . ."

Was she going to leave that sentence hanging again?

She wiped some tears. ". . . to be a huge success. Without our help."

Cameron closed his eyes. "Sometimes it's just nice to hear," he squeaked out before the tears came.

They stood there in a group hug, Cameron trying to breathe because he knew he'd need to be coherent at any moment.

"Dude!" came Spencer's voice not half a minute later.

Cameron wiped his eyes on his mom's shoulder before he looked up.

"I can't believe you," Spencer said. "I can't believe you threw away a million dollars."

"I got twenty-five thousand."

"It's not a million."

"I know," said Cameron, regaining his voice. "But I don't even know what a million dollars means. Anyway, I can live with myself. Could you live with yourself if you cheated someone out of that much money?"

"But it's a million dollars," Spencer said, his voice growing softer with each word. He said something else, but a metallic crash interrupted.

"Now, look what you've gone and done. Made me smash into the door frame," said the old man in the wheelchair. "Where are those two? Those two wonderful children?"

Carol ushered them over to the man who'd wheeled himself just inside the door.

He had a strong handshake. "Thaddeus G. Golliwop, the original," he said, and laughed. "Built this company with a nickel and an idea. And you two youngsters made me prouder than the proudest peacock today. I understand you're coming to my farm, spending a few days?"

Huh? Cameron looked at his parents. They were smiling.

Bert Golliwop stepped in. "They don't know about that yet, Dad."

"Woo-hoo! I love surprises! Surprise! I have a small parcel of land about an hour away from here. My farm. Thought all eight of you—"

"Ten, Dad. There were ten finalists."

"The more the merrier. But you'll be my guests while the foolhardy folks get this TV show together. A grand celebration!" He turned his wheelchair. "See you soon!"

Carol stepped up. "You won't be baling hay or anything. It's a resort. Swimming pools. Lake. Boats. Bicycles. Hiking trails. Arcade. Catered food. The whole works. Just for a week. No one else there except the ten of you, your families, and a few people from last year who can tell you what to expect."

Just hours later the helicopters to the resort left in pairs, heading into the setting sun. Cameron and his family were escorted from the landing pad to a four-bedroom house stocked with everything they hadn't known they'd need to pack.

First thing Cameron did was shower. Then he lay down on his bed for just a few minutes.

The knocking came way too soon. Didn't Spencer have a clue what he'd been through? "Go away, Spencer."

"It's not Spencer," said his mom. "You need to come out here."

He tried to open his eyes, but it was way too bright.

"And, Cameron?" she called. "Don't come out in your underwear."

Why was all this light coming through the window? He rolled over and looked at the clock: 9:17? In the morning? And what was wrong with his underwear?

Wait? Where was he?

He shot out of bed. The helicopter. The Games. The disaster. A future of facing ridicule for throwing away all that money. Maybe he could go back to sleep. Maybe he could sleep through seventh grade.

"Cameron?" said his mom again. This didn't sound like a breakfast call.

"Be out in a minute." He brushed his teeth, washed his pits, and ran his fingers through his hair. He put on new clothes from the closet. He heard chuckles through the doors. And a strange voice.

In the living room some man had Spencer doubled over in laughter.

The man stood. "So you're the freak who turned down a million dollars?"

Coming from this guy, whoever he was, it sounded more funny than stupid.

Cameron nodded. "That would be me." But how'd he know? "How'd you know?"

"It's next Thursday already," said the man. "Everyone knows." He laughed. Then he came and shook Cameron's hand. "My very good friends the Golliwops told me a little story about you, and as long as I was passing through—" He paused and looked at Cameron's dad. "Is it passing through when they send a plane to pick you up and fly you here?"

Cameron's dad shook his head.

"So I wasn't passing through. I was actually very busy in Los Angeles, and I haven't even bothered to introduce myself." He shook Cameron's hand. "Ever see the movie based on DoomTomb? Or the one based on Tell Me a Lie?"

"Everyone's seen those."

"Those are mine. I make movies. Roscoe Grant. Pleased to meet you."

Cameron felt himself stagger back an inch. Roscoe Grant? Here?

"So Bert Golliwop told me something about your wanting your videos to get noticed?"

Cameron nodded.

"You *are* the strong, silent type. I can't cure that, but I can help you with your video wish. Think you might have time to come to Hollywood the week after next? Shadow me for a few days? Show me what you can do, so I can show you how to do it better?"

Roscoe Grant handed Cameron a piece of paper. "Here's everything you need to know. Meanwhile," he said, pointing to a wrapped package near the door, "something for you to play with. See you soon!" And he left.

Cameron gently, methodically opened the box. No surprise what was inside, but this video camera had cost thousands and thousands of dollars.

"I'm going to Hollywood," he said.

CHAPTER 33

With thoughts of Hollywood dangling in front of his nose, Cameron was ready to leave the "farm." That wasn't an option. It had nothing to do with dragging Spencer and Walker away from the Cannonball Competitions or his dad from the gourmet cooking classes or his mom from the waterskiing. It was the final rule.

At first it seemed lame, especially when they had Lavinia talk to him about facing the world after coming in second. She couldn't know how he felt. No one could. He supposed, though, this was part of Golly's mandatory class, How to Act like a Normal Person When Your Entire Life Has Been Broadcast All Over the World.

After a while, though, he had to admit she made sense. "If you do only one thing," she said, "be prepared with answers. You'll hear all sorts of advice on what you could have done differently, and it's easy to get defensive and give snarky replies. Like, 'Let's see you get as far as I did.' And 'If you want to see how easy it is, strip to your underwear and sit in the school cafeteria taking a test you never studied for.'"

After that they had a good time coming up with lines no one should use. Everyone around the pool joined in. And the days pretty much flew like that, most of the time, just hanging around, getting to really know the rest of the contestants, this year's and last year's, in a normal—well, noncompetitive— setting. Except Rocky, who wasn't there, and Thorn, who, for some reason, seemed to be wherever Cameron wasn't.

The Gollywhopper Games were to air on TV two consecutive nights. The Golly people held a premiere party at the farm's theater with red carpet and fancy clothes for the first night's episode, which showed the regionals and the Stadium Round. But the second night before airtime, the contestants and their families had already boarded planes. The plan was to whisk them home before the credits rolled.

It's not that Cameron and his family missed seeing the show. Golly had loaded the private plane with a DVD. Cameron prayed they'd skip over his throwing away the million dollars, but they showed everything. He would have won if there'd been a different picture on the ceiling.

Now, though, he had nothing to hide.

They got home about an hour before the show ended. Already there were thirty-five messages on their answering machine; all the so-excitings and congratulations and I-don't-know-what-you-won-yet-Camerons, but-could-you-give-me-a-thousand-dollars-hahahas.

Cameron would have been fine without seeing the Games on TV again, but Walker had turned it on. It was at the part in the Rainbow Maze where they found their first packs.

"I don't get something," said Walker. "Why did you always go the wrong way after you picked up the packs? Didn't you see the arrow?"

"What arrow?"

"The packs were arranged in an arrow to show you which way to go."

"They were? Who told you that?"

"No one did," said Walker. "I saw it on the monitors when you were running it."

Cameron laughed. "If you keep noticing stuff like that, maybe you'll win the million dollars in two years." He nudged Walker, then headed to his room, where his life would be almost normal.

Golly had arranged for a team of guards to keep anyone away for the next forty-eight hours, which was great. Cameron wanted just one quiet night in his own bed before he faced the barrage of people who, according to last year's contestants, would come.

He downed a handful of the sweet 'n' salty snack mix from the giant food basket Golly had sent them and—

Doorbell? Hadn't the guards guaranteed no one would bother them?

Might as well get this over with. Cameron peeked around the corner, where he could hear and see everything but be mostly invisible himself.

One of the guards handed Cameron's dad a phone. "It's Mr. Golliwop."

"I understand," said his dad. "No problem, but why?" Pause. "Really?" Pause. He motioned for Cameron. "Absolutely!" Pause. "And yes, we do. Thank you!" He handed the phone back to the guard and held the door open for three camera people.

"What's going on?" asked Cameron's mom.

Their phone rang. His dad hit the speakerphone button. "Hello?"

"This is the White House operator calling for Cameron Schein. Is he there?"

Cameron nodded.

Spencer nudged him.

"Um, yes. This is Cameron."

"Please hold for the president of the United States."

"The who?"

His dad nodded. "This isn't a joke."

And it wasn't. It was the president's voice. "My family and I were sitting here watching the show tonight, and we kept shaking our heads, saying, 'Who does this? What kind of person turns down a million dollars?' We wanted to find out who."

"I guess I do?" said Cameron.

The president laughed. "There are few people

with the integrity to turn down that much money, Cameron, and that's why we want to meet you. We'd like you to come to the White House for lunch next week if you could find the time. Golly Toy and Game Company will pay your way here, and we'll treat you right. Would you do that?"

Would he? Um, yeah. "Yes, sir," he said.

"We'll get that all arranged, then. And thank you, Cameron. It's an honor."

Cameron was still reeling when he went to bed. This would not be a normal night. He tossed and turned and got up and paced and maybe fell asleep around three in the morning.

Again he woke to pounding on his door. He was about to yell at Spencer, but maybe it wasn't Spencer. It could have been the king of Denmark, the way things had been going. "Yeah?"

"Dude!" It was Spencer after all. "Get up! You're trending!"

"I'm what?"

"You're trending. Online. Everyone's talking about you." He barged in, pulled Cameron out of bed, and dragged him by his T-shirt to the computer.

"It's Clio," said Walker, who'd joined them. "She started it."

"Started what?"

"Dude," said Spencer, "she wanted to give you half her money, but they'd make her forfeit everything if she did, so she did this instead."

"Did what?"

"She got your whole team together. Last year's people, too. Bianca sends you hugs and kisses by the way, but they're all over the Internet, trying to get a million people to each send you one dollar."

Walker grabbed the mouse. "And look! People are already doing it." He clicked to a picture of a girl stuffing a dollar into an envelope addressed to Cameron in care of Golly Toy and Game Company. Then he clicked to another picture. "It's Thorn, and he's sending ten thousand dollars!"

"Why would he do that?" Cameron said. "Why would anyone? I'm not a charity case."

"Listen to you," said Spencer. "Such a doofus. You turned yourself into a hero. You're going to be a millionaire after all."

He was? "I am?"

"You are," said Walker.

He was? But with everything else that had happened, all the people he was going to meet, all the opportunities coming his way, did it matter now? Did all that money matter?

Maybe it did. Or not.

He'd figure it out, one step at a time.

Acknowledgments

This page starts with the usual thank-yous, but ends with the reason these particular acknowledgments even exist.

Thanks, first, to my Greenwillow editor, Virginia Duncan, who has given me this gift to write more episodes of *The Gollywhopper Games*. She took a simple comment from me ("I'm in the mood to write another contest book") and turned it into one of the best rides of my life. Thanks to her, too, I am privileged to work with the amazing Sarah Thomson, who really gets me, gets my characters, and gets a huge gold star for tugging on my sleeve to pull out the best of this story. My gratitude extends throughout the Greenwillow family to Lois Adams, who fielded my copyediting issues with patience, generosity, and overall loveliness; to Paul Zakris, who brilliantly handled the overall graphic elements, the cover design (fabulous art by Max Kostenko!), and who allowed me a sneak peek (though maybe he wishes he hadn't) at the interior illustrations by the talented Victoria Jamieson (Vicki, you're terrific!). Thanks also to those who have worked so hard behind the scenes of these chapters.

It's impossible to let go and write the fun parts unless you're surrounded by family and friends who make your life as carefree as possible. Thanks, specifically, to my husband, Dick, and his full-on support; to Cassie, who helps me find even more humor than I thought possible; and to Paige, whose amazing insights into my work help me realize the full story. And she doesn't think it's weird when I directly launch into character issues as if they were, in fact, real.

In that vein, thanks to my critique mates Cinda Chima, Debby Garfinkel, Martha Levine, Mary Beth Miller, and Kate Tuthill, who understand that it's kind to be cruel and who also make exploring random U.S. cities so much fun.

And always to Jennie Dunham, who deals with the business and leaves me free to imagine.

Now comes the thanks to those of you—and that probably IS you!—who have made these particular acknowledgments possible. In 2008, a brand-new book by an unknown author found its way into the world. One minute *The Gollywhopper Games* was walking side by side with a myriad of other titles, and the next, you gave it a chance. Whether you are a bookseller, a teacher, a librarian, a parent, or a reader(!); whether you borrowed *The Gollywhopper Games* or bought it for yourself or to share; or if you included it on a summer reading list; or read it to your class; or nominated it for your state reading awards; or reordered it for your store; whether you let me into your schools, your stores, your libraries, or your conferences; whether you wrote a report on it, made a video because of it, created your own puzzles, suggested it to one friend or dozens . . .

You provided the fuel to turn this little story into The Book That Could. It was only by your word of mouth that *The Gollywhopper Games* demanded a book two and a book three. And I will be grateful always.

The games continue. . . .
Read on for a sneak peek at

Friend or Foe

By Jody Feldman

To hear his friends describe it, it had been a thing of beauty—Zane's soaring sideways, in slow-motion they swore, to make an epic catch. Honestly? It had been stupidity. When the baseball shot the gap between second and third, Zane should have let it go. This was gym class, and this was *not* football. But his instincts had taken over, which caused his chin to hit the ground and his teeth to clank together.

Now at lunch, it was like his dizziness had teamed with the combo-smell of peanut butter, tuna fish, and French fries to create some super-scent. It weaseled up his nose and made the lights a little too bright; his turkey wrap, a little too salty; his friends, especially, a little too loud. It was like he could feel his brain and not in a good way.

His core group was deep in joke mode with the doofus managers of their football team, Thing 1 and Thing 2, who were sitting at their table today. Zane was spacing out on the conversation, but he knew the JZs—Jamaal, Jerome, Julio, and Zack—were using the Things to set up another inside gag. The Things deserved it. They always bragged that they were the heart of the team, but they pretty much stood around laughing at their own lame jokes until Coach yelled at them to do their jobs. Right now, though, none of it was amusing. Zane wanted to find a bed and rest his brain.

At least these symptoms felt different from last November's, and he could name the months of the year backward; even so, he needed to prove to himself that the headache and the overly bright lights were born from fear, just fear, because Zane could not afford another concussion.

He zeroed in on the conversation and stayed with it the rest of lunch. He nailed the vocab quiz in CommArts. He *habla*'d *español* when he was asked. But his head was still clouding as Mr. Longley droned on about the freezing point in Celsius. He propped his chin with his hand, willing the steady pressure to get him through this last half hour. Then he'd go home, rest—

Bzzz! Bzzz!

Thirty minutes already? Had he passed out? No one was rushing the door, everyone was asking about the buzzer, and the clock itself had barely moved. Zane breathed.

"And now we come to what promises to be an unfortunate waste of time." Mr. Longley held up a thick, yellow envelope. "I have no idea what this is, nor its purpose, but when I hand out these sheets"— he paused to read the writing on the envelope— "'You will have ten minutes to turn them over and complete as many questions as you can. Please put your answers in the blanks provided. You may use the margins of the paper as work space. If you can't figure out an answer, skip the question. This will not be graded; this will not go on your permanent record.'"

He looked up from the envelope, over his glasses. "This will, however, take valuable time from the seventh grade curriculum." He slapped a paper on each desk. "Put your name on the side where it says 'Name.'

You'd think, by now, we wouldn't need to tell you that. When I say go, turn the paper over and begin."

Zane would go. He would answer these questions. All of them. That would prove his brain wasn't bleeding, that he could play spring football, that he wouldn't be sidelined forever.

"Go!"

Zane turned over his paper. Math!

Question #1
* * * * * * * * * * *

Bob ordered a pizza with 48 pieces of pepperoni at 10 cents apiece, 30 pieces of sausage at 14 cents apiece, 26 pieces of green pepper at 6 cents apiece, three different types of cheese at $1.28 per type, and the $3.89 medium crust. The sauce was free.

Zane stopped to calculate the pepperoni and sausage. If he could do that in his head, he was probably fine. Okay. Four dollars and eighty cents in pepperoni. Then thirty times fourteen which—

His eye caught the last sentence of the question.

Write an A if Bob is an omnivore;
B if he's a herbivore;
or C if he's a carnivore. _____

A. $18.19

B. $18.39

C. $17.19

D. $18.29

Since when had Zane forgotten to read the entire thing? Since the dive? He wrote *A*.

Question #2
* * * * * * * * * * *

If you eliminate one letter from each name below, the remaining letters, in order, will spell a common word. Rearrange the eliminated letters to spell another common word. _____

Alice

Peter

Clement

Dewey

Albert

Rearrange letters with a rearranged brain?

He'd try. If he got rid of the *A* in Alice . . .

Okay. That was a word. Next. If he dropped the *P* in Peter, it'd be *eter*. No. The *E*? *Pter* sounded like someone spitting. The *T*! Next. Clement. Not the *C*. Not the *L*. Yes, the *L*. Not so hard, at least so far. Next. Dewey. Either *ewey, dwey, deey, dewy,* or *dewe. Dewy*? Filled with dew? That was the only one that seemed remotely right.

So far, the dropped letters could spell *late*, but he still needed one more. Not the *A* in Albert. Not the *L*. The *B*! L-A-T-E plus a *B*. *Blate*? *Bleat*? Was that what sheep did? Or was that spelled with two *E*s? *Belat. Betal*, like petal? Maybe it started with a *T*. A lot of words did. And a lot of words ended in *—le*. Or *—ble*? That was it! *Table.*